NICK & CO TO THE RESCUE

The gang is back! Despite their good
intentions anything involving Nick and
Co. seems to lead to trouble.

In this latest adventure the start of
term sees them trying to save their
school *and* on the trail of a con man. Then
there's some dirty work in a local cycle
race . . .

"Life is going to be busy . . ." reflects
Nick in a rare quiet moment. How right
he is!

Bob Croson, the author, is married to
Jean, an artist, and they have two
teenage sons, Bill and Ben.

Bob is a General Primary Adviser in
Derbyshire.

NICK
& CO
TO THE RESCUE

Bob Croson

A LION PAPERBACK
Oxford · Batavia · Sydney

Copyright © 1990 Bob Croson

Published by
Lion Publishing plc
Sandy Lane West, Oxford, England
ISBN 0 7459 1832 8
Albatross Books Pty Ltd
PO Box 320, Sutherland, NSW 2232, Australia
ISBN 0 7324 0222 0

First edition 1990
Reprinted 1992

British Library Cataloguing in Publication Data
Croson, Bob, *1946–*
    Nick & Co to the rescue.
    I. Title
    823'.914 [J]

    ISBN 0-7459-1832-8

Printed and bound in Great Britain
by Cox & Wyman Ltd, Reading

Contents

1

Collision Course

"Go . . ."

The mayor lowered his starter's flag and we were off. Hurtling into the park, pushing our "brilliant" go-kart, racing against the other teams for the best track before the course narrowed down to the path that went right round Broad Meadows Park.

"Push. PUSH. Pu-ush," I screamed at my team, trying to get them to build up speed as fast as possible.

Sparky, my best pal, sat in the kart trying to keep hold of the steering wheel as he was bounced about. Of course, I was in charge, Nick Baker, the leader of the world famous "Nick & Co."

"Are you OK?" I yelled at Sparky.

"O-o-o-o-ooo, k-k-k-kay!," he answered back. I think that meant he was all right, but we couldn't stop now, so he had to be.

Broad Meadows is a huge park, with playing areas, sports grounds, a small lake, some gardens, and a wood, and it was going to be a hard push to be first team round and win the prize.

This first bit was a mad dash, with everybody possible pushing to get in the lead before the narrower path was reached.

The race was for all the kids from our part of the city and was taking place right at the end of our summer holiday. There were all sorts of teams, but I was keeping my eye on one in particular. That was "Ram's Gang". He was my dreaded enemy both in class and on the street. However hard I tried to like other people, there was always Ram to come along, do something horrible, and make me lose my "cool". I watched him like a hawk!

His team was trying hard to reach the path first. I could see them drawing alongside us. Ram had an evil smirk on his face. I knew that he was going to try to knock us out somehow. Each time they drew near I screamed at my team to "PUSH HARDER!!", and we managed to get away.

If only we could last a bit further we would be away on the path where it would be harder for Ram to cause trouble.

They were alongside us again and lurching towards us. Ram kicked out and just missed one of our team, Whizzer. He tried again, kicking out with his foot. I was ready for him! I reached out with my arm and pulled, timing it beautifully.

The effect was dramatic. The kart he was pushing slewed round, and he and the rest of his gang joined him in a great heap on the grass.

"I'll get you for this!" Ram screamed as he staggered to his feet.

But we were well away, they'd never catch us now. I smiled and waved, and he shook his fist back. Boy, did it feel good to get one over on Ram.

Our team, all from my class at school, with me in charge, was in the lead. Sparky was the driver because he was the lightest — and the toughest, apart from me, that is. Sparky lives next door to me, and he has a sister, Samantha — Sam for short — who is — er — a special friend of mine. She was pushing the kart next to me. Also at the back was Raj, a brilliant sportsman and the brightest of all of us. His full name is Rajinder Singh Chopra, but everybody calls him Raj.

We were getting near to where the path narrowed and everything was going great. "This is going to be easy," I yelled at Sam. "Nigel Mansell in the cockpit's doing all right as well."

We both laughed. But I had spoken too soon!

The rest of the team were pushing on the sides. To one side was Whizzer, who is very athletic. He goes everywhere with headphones and a "Walkman", listening to reggae and hip-hop, so he tends to be in a world of his own.

On the other side were Chip, our computer whiz-kid, whose dad was the first black teacher at our school, and Lump who was the largest, if not the fittest, member of the gang. Chip's real name is Norman, and Lump's is Franco. His dad owns the local chip shop, "Granellis". They both hate physical exercise of any sort, and this was no exception. They had to be "persuaded" to join in!

Near to where the race joined the main path round the park, it was obvious that Whizzer, Chip and Lump would have to break off to allow the kart through the narrow gap between the lake and the wood.

At least it would have been obvious to any normal human being — but not to those three plonkers.

Whizzer was miles away, absorbed in his own music, pushing hard but totally unaware of his surroundings. Lump and Chip were too busy grumbling and arguing with each other to notice where they were going.

I yelled at Whizzer. He smiled and waved back! One of these days I'm going to jump on that stupid Walkman of his.

I tried Lump and Chip, but couldn't attract their attention either. They were trying hard not to look at me because they thought I would only be yelling at them to push harder.

Suddenly Chip saw the danger and leaped out of the way at the last moment — unfortunately straight in front of Lump, who proceeded to complete a beautiful swallow dive — worth at least 5.6 for artistic merit in any Olympic competition — into the shallow end of the park lake.

At the same moment Whizzer at last noticed where he was going. He athletically hurdled a small fence, dodged in and out of the trees in the wood like an American footballer, and scored a touchdown with his Walkman somewhere near the park pavilion.

We couldn't stop!

"Catch us up," I yelled to them all as we sped on.

Raj, Sam and I pushed and pushed, longing for a downhill bit, and even though we were getting out of breath we managed to build up another gap. I just hoped the other three would get sorted out and catch up with us. I didn't know how long we could keep this up.

Looking back I could see Ram's team barging and battling its way through the other karts.

At last we reached a long downhill part of the path which ended in a sharp turn round the back of the children's playground. Soon the kart was going faster than we could push. I jumped on the back; Sam and Raj cut across to meet us at the end of the play area.

"This is great!" I yelled to Sparky, who thumbed up in return.

We were going really fast now and getting near the bend. Sparky and I had practised this for ages; I set myself to lean across and keep the weight on the inside wheels.

Then I noticed something! The nut that kept the back wheel on was nearly off. This couldn't be. I had checked it myself. Before I had time to do anything or warn Sparky, we were at the corner, the wheel came off, the axle hit the ground and started making sparks. Sparky tried to control it but we slewed off the path and hit the soft grass.

The axle dug in, and I was thrown off, rolling on the ground until I came to a stop.

An old man who had been watching rushed over.

"Are you all right?" I yelled at Sparky.

"Yes", came the muffled reply, "but get this thing off me."

The old man and I pulled the kart off and Sparky sat up. He seemed OK except for his leg, which was grazed raw.

Sam and Raj arrived, closely followed by Whizzer, Chip, and a dripping Lump. Just at that moment Ram's kart came past, too, with him on top, laughing and pointing at us. That really made me mad!

My gang are part of our local church youth club, led by the curate, Doug. Right now, the feelings I had towards Ram were not very Christian at all. I would have liked to punch him on the nose!

I thought quickly!

"Raj, find the nut for the wheel. Chip, get the wheel," I ordered. "Sparky, will you be all right?"

He nodded.

We banged the kart back together again and, leaving Sparky behind, with Sam in the driving seat, we set off in pursuit.

We were last now, but I was determined and we were the fastest team by far. Soon we were fighting our way back through the field. Round the back of the sports field we forced our way through to second spot, with only Ram's team in front. One last effort from everyone and we just might catch them on the last straight.

I could see they were tiring, but I could also see the finishing line ahead.

"PUSH," I screamed. "PUSH, PUSH HARDER!!"

2
Pipped at the Post

We hurtled across the finishing line and collapsed in a heap.

Second! We had nearly caught up with Ram's kart, but they had just managed to beat us!

"Had a few problems?" Ram called across to us, with a stupid smirk on his face.

I didn't answer; I was too out of breath. By the time I had recovered and thought of something to say, Ram was out of earshot. Instead, I turned on the rest of the gang. "You bunch of useless idiots," I groaned. "Look at you, wet, muddy, brainless . . ."

"Hang on a minute," Sam butted in. "It wasn't our fault that the wheel fell off. After all, you insisted on being in charge of building the kart, and you said it was the best-designed kart you'd ever seen!"

"Yes," Chip joined in. "Ram said it was, too."

We all fell silent and turned to him as he blundered on.

"He said," continued Chip, innocently, "that

nothing could ever beat it."

I had a nasty feeling growing inside!

"When did Ram say this?" I asked quietly.

"Before the race," Chip went on. "You know, when I was looking after the kart while you walked round a bit of the course. It was just before I went to the toilet."

We all looked at him.

The light suddenly dawned in his eyes.

"But I had to go. I was desperate!" he whined, realizing what he had done.

"You Wally!" I yelled at him.

My dog, Wally, leapt at me in instant obedience, landing me in the mud again. Nobody dared to laugh!

"Not you, Wally. Get off," I shouted at my over-affectionate and slightly stupid pet.

Somebody laughed.

It was Ram.

"Cheats never prosper," I grunted at him.

"You just can't stand being beaten by somebody better," he responded.

"You only won because you fiddled with the wheel of our kart," I shouted back, standing up. I was beginning to get steamed up. Inside, my "temper control switch" was beginning to blow.

Ram wasn't going to back off either. He stepped forward menacingly. "Prove it," he growled.

"Chip saw you," I responded, not quite truthfully, and stepped nearer to him.

Ram took another step forward and raised his fist.

Wally took action! He may not be very big. He may look a bit odd. But, boy, has he got a sharp set of teeth. Wally went for Ram's ankle as if it were his favourite bone!

"Yeeooow!" Ram yelped. His response was to kick Wally so hard that he skidded across the mud, whining as he slid!

Just as Wally turned for another go and I was about to land a punch on Ram's nose, Sparky stepped in.

He had limped the short way back, helped by Bert, the man who had been watching at the accident.

"Hold on, hold on," Sparky demanded. He turned to me, "Now cool it, Nick, this isn't doing any good."

I could feel anger bubbling up inside. It was so hard to stop.

"Ram, why don't you go away?" Sparky added. "You've caused enough damage for one day."

Realizing that there were too many people about, plus a dog, he backed off and walked away, with a final "You've not heard the last of this, Nick Baker."

I was about to reply, when Sparky stopped me. Little Mo, my young sister, had grabbed Wally, and the others gathered round. I was still very worked up inside.

"I don't know," grumbled Bert. "Young people these days. Just don't know how to behave."

My fuse blew! I knew it was wrong but the

old bad Nick won the day. "Do you mean me?" I demanded, turning on him.

"I speak as I find," he replied.

"Well, I speak as I find," I went on, out of control. "And I find too many people like to tell me what's right and what isn't, usually without finding out all the facts."

Sparky jumped, well, hopped between us.

"Er, Bert, thanks ever so much for your help," he said. "Nick doesn't mean all that, he's just upset at losing the race."

Sam dragged me away, as Bert left in the opposite direction, muttering about how rude young people were these days.

The "red mist" of stupid anger began to go. I still felt pretty steamed up, but I was calm enough to help Sam take Sparky home to get his injuries cleaned up. The others were going to take our battered kart to the club hut and meet Sam and me there.

At the hut, Doug was waiting for us. As I've said, he's the curate of the local church, our youth club leader, and a really great guy, in spite of being a grown-up!

The rest of the gang had told him all about what had happened, but I told him my version in case they had got the facts wrong. He let me talk, adding those little questions and comments that made me realize what a plonker I was:

"Wasn't Bert kind to help Sparky? Didn't Chip

and Lump do well, when it wasn't their sort of thing? Did you thank Bert for his help? Did you thank the rest of the gang for their help when you got the prize for the best-looking kart?"

Why does he always know how to get at a bloke? My anger was changing to a sort of embarrassed sick feeling inside.

A few months before, I had made up my mind to go along with Doug and his lot and be a real Christian. To begin with it was all dead easy. I was sort of carried away with the enthusiasm of it all. Even my mum noticed the difference when I helped with the washing up! But now, all the bad old ways kept slipping back, and I was finding it hard not to give in.

Doug didn't say anything more, but I knew what he was thinking, and I just dried up in an embarrassed silence.

Thankfully Doug changed the subject. He started talking about all the plans for the autumn in our club and church. We were going on lots of trips, and had entered some competitions, including a cycle race that sounded great.

We were also going to help at some church services. They were good fun. I never would have believed that I might enjoy going to church, but at this one the people were so happy and friendly with each other, it took away all the stuffiness that had always put me off. I wasn't so sure about one thing that Doug suggested. There was going to be a joint venture between the town's churches and schools to help the local

Senior Citizens. It was called "Reaching Across Generations" — another of those titles thought up by grown-ups in a meeting. You know, they sit around for hours just thinking up titles for things, then what do they come up with — RAG! If they think I'm going to walk around with that on a T-shirt, they'd better think again.

"What if you finish up helping Bert?" Sam said, with a cheeky grin.

I gave her a look!

It was more fun talking about the cycle race. The race was to be sponsored by the cycle shop next to our school, and the owner of the shop, Mr Bolton, (the chairperson of our school governors) was going to present a trophy: "The Bolton Trophy".

We were going to win! That would make up for the kart race. It was a team race, so there would have to be some planning. I would be best at that! Mind you, looking at the assortment of bashed up bikes that we rode home on, I was beginning to have my doubts.

Eventually, only Sam and I were left. We were having a ride round before we went in. I enjoyed Sam's company. She is tough and strong, and can outrun and out-think most of my other pals. We were riding about and talking about this and that when suddenly we heard a shout. Rounding a corner we almost fell over an old lady who was sitting on the pavement outside her home crying.

"He's . . . taken . . . my . . . money," she sobbed.

Sam leapt off her bike and put an arm round the old lady.

"Go and get your dad," she said to me. "I'll take her inside."

While Sam helped the old lady to her feet, I made off home on my bike. My dad is a policeman, which has its problems for me sometimes.

When we returned, the lady said a man had told her that he'd come to read her meter. But when he had gone, she realized that her purse had been taken, with all her savings. I really felt sorry for her, she was so upset. I made up my mind to catch whoever had done such an awful thing.

Little did I know that this would mean another adventure for Nick & Co.

3

Running into Trouble

Back to school . . . Ugh!

This was the worst day of the year. Starting back after the summer break is positively the most drastically awful experience known to human beings . . . and probably Martians as well!

First there is "getting up". Now, if we were going on a trip to the seaside, I would be up before dawn, bright as a button and badgering everybody to get going. But getting up for school is something else. I just can't seem to wake up. My whole body is weighted down to the bed. And I know I'm not the only one! I wonder if it's some sort of disease. I'm surprised that nobody's found a cure for it yet. My dad reckons he has, but I don't think a cold sponge down the back of the pyjamas is a very scientific approach, and I threatened to report him to the NSPCC if he did it again!

This time I got out of bed without Dad's shock treatment. I managed to force down two bowls of cornflakes and three pieces of toast in the five minutes available, and hurtled out to meet Sparky and Sam.

We live next door to each other, and usually fall out on to the street at about the same time. As usual, we were on the last minute and had to run to get to school on time. Sparky, Sam and I are good runners and we usually made a race of it. It also helped us to wake up.

I was determined to win and set off at a terrific pace. Hurtling round the corners and down the streets I managed to keep a good distance in front.

People are a bit like cars. The faster they go, the longer it takes to stop! Nick Baker is no exception and is also a genius at getting in to trouble! Put the two together and this is what you get.

Next to the school is Mr Bolton's Cycle Shop. Being the chairperson of the school governors, he likes to be there on the first day of term, so just before school starts he leaves his wife in charge of the shop and makes his way to school.

Now, my route to school involves a tight double turn round the cycle shop and into the school drive. Nigel Mansell would have made it easily, passing slower "vehicles" with no trouble. Not me! And, if you're going to get it wrong, why not do it in style!

I hurtled round the corner of the shop and came to a "slower vehicle", Mr Bolton, too late to take avoiding action. Actually I was shouting back at the others to say that they stood no chance of catching me. I got as far as, "You'll never catch me now . . . oww!'', as I careered at top speed into him.

He didn't fall over; I did. I bounced off his stomach like the steel ball in a pinball machine and landed hard on the pavement. But he wasn't concerned at all about whether I was hurt.

"You stupid boy," was all he said. "There could have been a nasty accident."

"There was," I muttered, rubbing my knee.

"What was that?" he asked as Sparky and Sam arrived. "Are you being cheeky?"

"I don't think so," Sparky quickly butted in. "He's just hurt his knee a little."

I wanted to say more but Sam was digging me hard in the back. A signal to shut up.

Mr Bolton took my name and said, "The headmaster will hear about this."

On top of all that it made us late and we got a detention each. What a start to the term!

Then I had to face Ram. Most of my class were great, but Ram and his mates were just awful.

Ram didn't waste a second.

"Good evening," he said as we walked through the door. "Frightened to face me then? Can't face defeat?"

"I can face cheats any time," I responded sharply.

"Er, excuse me," interrupted Miss Nolan, our form teacher. "But could you continue your philosophical debate another time? I should like to finish registration."

Why do teachers like to use "posh" words

23

when they're telling us something? It's probably because they want to make sure we understand that they are more clever than us!

As we filed to the first assembly of the school year Ram was getting at me all the way. Sam and Sparky kept pulling me away, and Miss Nolan was doing what teachers do in such situations, shouting at anyone and everyone.

In assembly "Potty" Potter, our headteacher, welcome us all back, then handed over to Mr Bolton who "droned on" for hours. He really liked the sound of his own voice, which was just as well because nobody else listened. I spent most of the time returning Ram's glares.

There was a bit of religious chat from "Potty", about doing good this term and being kind to each other. I hoped the teachers were listening!

Everything was passing as usual, hymn and all, when I was suddenly jolted out of my doze.

"Would Nicholas Baker please go to my room after assembly," announced Potty.

Everyone turned and stared at me. I went bright red.

Ram smirked.

As we all filed out of the hall I turned in the direction of Potty's office. I knew why I was going there, old Bolthead must have demanded action for getting in my way earlier. I stood round the corner from Potty's door to wait.

It wasn't long before he appeared.

He wasn't alone!

He was with Bolthead, and they were so busy

talking that they hardly noticed me. All I got was, "Wait there!" from Potty.

I waited until they were round the corner, then followed. Whatever they were talking about sounded very interesting, so I just sort of "happened" to find myself near the slightly open door of Potty's office.

I thought Mr Potter got cross only with kids, but he was really going on at Mr Bolton. And what he was saying was amazing. Potty was complaining about the school being closed down and everybody being transferred to other schools because the numbers had gone down. He was saying how wrong it was and how difficult it would be for the children at the school.

Mr Bolton was going on about how it had to be done, and there was no point in trying to stop it. They were getting really steamed up. You know, it's what grown-ups call a heated discussion. When it's between kids, it's a row and you get told off for doing it.

Mr Bolton left, giving me just enough time to get back round the corner. He was so mad he didn't notice me.

"Enter," called Potty.

I expected to get a real ticking off with him being in such a bad mood!

"Ah, Baker," he said as I crept through the door.

"You had a little, er, trouble with Mr Bolton I hear," he went on.

I didn't say anything, just waited for the voice

to change to "shout" mode, you know, the nose-to-nose "discussion" with only one speaker! But it didn't happen!

"Perhaps you could be a little more careful when you are negotiating that particular bend," was all he said in a quiet voice.

Then he winked, and said, "Right, off you go now."

Well, you could have knocked me down with a chicken feather. I wondered what would have happened if he hadn't just had a "ding-dong" with Bolthead, then left quickly before he changed his mind.

By now it was morning break, so I went straight out into the yard, slowly beginning to take in what had happened. I was walking over to the rest of the gang when suddenly there was a jolt from the side. That rat Ram had come up behind me and barged past.

"Oh, sorry," he smirked. "Didn't notice you. Had a bit of bother then?"

I was getting really fed up with Ram, and it was still only day one of term!

"Look you," I started. "If you don't quit bothering me I am going to forget myself and belt you one."

"You and whose army?" was his reply.

I could feel my hand curling up in to a fist. It had been one of those days and I was getting fed up.

"Right . . ." I replied, and moved closer.

Before I got any further Sam and Sparky butted

in. Sparky dragged me away, and Sam told Ram to "Push off and wind somebody else up."

Quick as a flash, Ram had his pals round him. "Need your girlfriend to rescue you?" he yelled, for everybody to hear.

Boy, sometimes it was so hard to do the right thing. I just wanted to have a go at him, but I knew that it would do no good. Fortunately the bell went and we had to go indoors, because I was just about at the end of my tether.

On the way in Sparky asked me how I had got on, so I told him and the rest of the gang about what I had overheard.

They were shocked. What would happen to us all?

On top of that, how was I going to get through this terrible first day?

4
Nothing but Trouble

English is sort of "middle yuk". On the scale between Games, which is great, and Maths, which is "mega yuk", it falls about halfway. But today, even with Miss Nolan as our teacher, I was dreading it.

I just didn't know how I was going to get to the end of the day without doing something to Ram. I knew he would try to set me up as well and that made it even worse.

I was right. As soon as we were sitting down, Ram was whispering comments about how I hid behind my girlfriend.

I could feel the back of my neck going red, and Ram knew he was getting to me. He just kept on with the whispering and teasing. Finally I could stand it no longer and turned round to give him a glare.

"Just belt up," I mouthed at him.

"Nick Baker," came the voice of Miss Nolan. "Will you turn round and get on with your work."

There isn't any justice. Teachers always get it

wrong, well, that's how I see it anyway! I didn't argue. What's the point? I just glared at Ram who was nearly falling off his chair in silent laughter.

But it didn't end there. A few minutes later Ram came past me to take his book out to the front, nudging me on the way and making me smudge my work.

On the way back I couldn't resist the temptation and caught him with my elbow. I didn't do it fiercely, but the way Ram reacted it was like he was poleaxed. He collapsed in a heap, clutching the side of his leg in agony.

I had been stitched up good and proper!

"What on earth's happened?" Miss Nolan demanded.

"Miss," Ram whined. "It's Baker, Miss, he's dead-legged me."

The lying toad, I hardly touched him.

"I hardly touched him Miss," I responded. But it was no use.

"I'll see you after class," she said, staring crossly at me. Then to Ram, "Get up, it can't be that bad."

Ram staggered to his feet and limped over to his desk. Miss Nolan returned to the front. I turned to Ram, and he smirked back, the rat.

After class, everyone went out and I was left with Miss Nolan.

"Now look, Nick," she started. "You have made an awful start to the school year. One day and you're already in trouble with all sorts of people. I just hope . . ." I'd switched off. When teachers start on like this I start thinking of something else. They all say the same thing anyway. Like parents. So long as you nod and look sorry you're usually all right! I thought about what had happened in Potty's room and all about the school closing down. As much as I hated school, I wasn't at all keen on being moved somewhere else. This was my school. ". . . so let's think about starting again," Miss Nolan was still yapping on in teacher-speak!

"Er, Miss," I interrupted. "What do you know about the school closing?"

"How do you know about that?" she demanded, irritated that I hadn't really been listening to her ticking-off.

"Oh, I just happened to hear something," I replied vaguely.

"Well, you weren't supposed to," she responded.

I just looked at her.

There was a pause.

"Look Nick," she went on. "Just be patient, you'll find out in time. Then you may be able to get your parents to do something. But for now keep your nose out, or you might find yourself in even more trouble."

I just looked at her again.

"Oh, go on, get off," she finally said. "And stay out of trouble . . . if you can." I actually managed to get through the rest of the day without getting in to any more bother, a miracle of answered prayer. Not mine but Sparky's and

Sam's. I was too busy thinking about what I had heard, and I find thinking very hard. My dad reckons I find it impossible, judging from my exam results.

The next day in school we had PE. My favourite.

However there was a new PE teacher, a Mr Pick! He sounded horrible. He was. We took one look at him and suddenly went off PE. He was tough-looking but small, with sharp features and a long nose. And he didn't smile.

"Hurry up and get changed," he barked. "And we'll see what you're made of."

I didn't like the sound of that.

We changed quickly and lined up in the gym.

Ram was too busy sizing up this new bloke to cause us any trouble.

"I think we shall call this one 'nose-pick'," I whispered to Lump, as much to cheer him up as anything, because he looked frightened to death by our new teacher.

"You boys, be quiet," Mr Pick yelled at us. "I'll have no talking in gym."

Good grief, this guy was a right nutter!

"Right," Pick went on. "Today you are going to do some circuit training. I have set it out, as you can see, all you have to do is follow the arrows and the instructions. I shall start you in one minute intervals." And he did, to the second.

Lump and Chip were looking very pale. Raj

and Whizzer would be all right, they were very fit. So were Sparky and myself.

Sparky was going with Chip to help him, and I was going to try to help Lump round. By the time it was our turn, Lump was shaking like a leaf, terrified of both the circuit and Pick, who was shouting at everybody to get on with it.

First we had to do twenty-five step-ups on to a bench. Lump managed them, just! But he was already puffing and blowing, and his face was bright red. The further on we went, doing pull-ups, split jumps and all sorts of crazy things, the worse Lump was getting.

"I'm not going to make it," he whispered breathlessly to me, as he struggled with pull-ups, trying to get his chin up to the bar just once. He had so much weight to pull up it was almost impossible. I was also worried that if he once got up, he'd get his chin stuck and strangle himself!

"You'll make it," I whispered back. "Just keep going."

"I can't keep going," he gasped. "I'm going to die."

"Be quiet over there," Pick barked. "And get on with it."

Lump jumped in fear and waddled over to the next exercise, too frightened to argue. Press-ups!

I thought it would be a good idea to have a quiet chat to him to take his mind off his agony. Pick was busy getting Ram to do some "rabbit jumps". It was nice to see him suffering!

"Hey Lump," I whispered. "What do you make of the school closure business? I think we've got to do something."

"What?" gasped Lump.

"Well, first of all, the gang has got to form an action group, a protest group," I replied.

"Oh no," groaned Lump. "More trouble."

"You boys," yelled Pick. "Come here."

Lump looked as if he was going to be sick!

"Leave this to me," I muttered to him as we made our way over.

Lump didn't look confident.

"What are you talking about?" Pick demanded.

"Nothing much," I replied, as innocently as I could.

"Well it must have been something very important if you could spare some of your precious breath to say it," Pick replied. "So you'd better come out with it, or there will be a detention."

I already had one for being late on the first day, so I told him what we had been talking about. I thought he would be sympathetic. I couldn't have been more wrong.

"Well I think it's a good idea," he responded. "It would get some of you dumb, dirty and lazy inner-city types to learn from other kids in better areas. You might not be so badly behaved then. Your manners might improve." What a terrible thing to say! It wasn't worth answering back!

This time I wasn't going to get angry. I prayed

a silent prayer to God to help stop me getting steamed up.

"I was trying to help my pal," I said. "That seemed to me very good manners."

Pick was not amused. He thought I was being cheeky. I wasn't. Well, only a bit!

He made us both do an extra circuit and followed us round. I just made it, but Lump threw up all over Mr Pick's nice new trainers. What a pity!

Ram was waiting in the showers to take the opportunity to get me going.

"What a brilliant gang you've got," he teased. "Can't win races, can't take defeat, all fat, frightened and flabby."

I just couldn't handle this guy. I didn't want to stay calm. I wanted to get angry. I turned on him. Sparky stepped between us, together with Whizzer and Raj.

"Haven't you got anybody normal in your lot?" Ram went on.

I was ready to go for him but Sparky stopped me. "Cool it, Nick," Sparky said to me. "You'll only get us all in more bother. Get dressed and get out."

God has his ways of helping, even when you don't ask!

I took Sparky's advice. Ignoring Ram's taunts, I got dressed and left quickly with the rest of the gang. We walked down the corridor towards our next lesson, on the way bumping into Miss Nolan. She didn't look too pleased.

"I was looking for you lot," she said to us. "Mr Pick has been telling me that you have been in trouble again. Can't you ever behave?"

"But Miss . . ." I began.

"Look," she cut in. "It's just not good enough. I thought you were a reformed character Nick. You've told me that you go to church these days. Doesn't it make a difference? Shouldn't you start to act the way you talk?"

I was stunned to silence.

"That's a bit strong, Miss," Sparky chipped in. "It's not all Nick's fault."

Thanks a bunch Sparky, I thought. None of it was my fault the way I looked at it.

Miss Nolan didn't seem convinced.

I just walked off. I wasn't sure whether I was embarrassed or angry. It was always the same, I thought. Misunderstood, whatever I did and whichever way I tried. There isn't any justice! Should I give up, and go back to being the old Nick? It didn't seem to make much difference.

5

Lending a Hand

I don't understand grown-ups, especially teachers.

I certainly don't understand why keeping kids in is any use at all. First of all the teachers have to stay behind as well, which is like punishing themselves. They always look half dead after school anyway. I can't think why! It also seems a bit weird that you have to sit for an hour getting bored doing some boring work, when they spend most of the time trying to persuade you that learning is fun, interesting, and exciting!

I just don't understand.

Walking back from yet another hour spent in detention, together with Sam and Sparky, all for being two minutes late, we were chatting about things. I was complaining about how hard it was to be a Christian. "It's all right for you two," I complained. "You've had more practice. I'm just about ready to give up."

"Oh, don't be so daft," replied Sparky. "You're doing all right. It's not a blinking league table you know. There's no prize for who does best. It's nothing to do with that. Just stick at it."

I was feeling a bit sorry for myself, everybody seemed to be getting at me, so I wasn't really listening to Sparky.

"I just don't think it's for me," I went on. "I can't keep it up."

"Oh Nick," Sam joined in. "Nothing's changed. You still believe in God, don't you?"

"Yes," I replied.

"Well then," she went on. "Just remember what Doug said. You've got to trust. It's not a competition. Your trouble is that you always have to be top."

"Yes," Sparky continued. "And you're a rotten loser as well!"

"OK, OK," I replied. "I submit. I'll give it another go. Tell you what," I went on, "I'll race you home. Last one puts double the collection in next Sunday."

"Nick, you're hopeless," they both groaned. Then, realizing they were being teased, they started to chase me.

I ran ahead, laughing, looking back to see how far ahead I was. Suddenly I hit something soft, and bounced off on to the pavement. Here we go again! Apparently, this guy had come hurtling out of a house without looking! He didn't even stop to apologize, but ran on round the corner.

I was just beginning to pick myself up when I was bounced to the ground again. This time it was Bert, of all people, the old bloke who helped Sparky at the kart race.

I was staying down now until I was sure nobody else was going to knock me to the ground again. From my position down there I watched as Bert made off after the other bloke, waving his stick and shouting, "Stop thief!"

It didn't register to begin with, and by the time I realized what was happening the man was well away.

Sparky and Sam came along and picked me up, then they went to see if Bert was all right. They helped him back in to the house, then almost at once my dad screeched up in his police car.

Everything seemed to be happening very fast. All he said was, "What are you doing here?" as he dashed past me in to the house. I followed him.

Sparky and Sam had sat Bert down and given him a drink of water.

"What happened?" my dad asked Bert.

Bert told him that this man had knocked on his door saying he was from the council and had to check the safety of the electricity in the house. Bert had let him in and left him to it, then returned to find him going through his desk. Bert then threatened him with his stick and the man had run off.

"I would have caught him too if that lad hadn't got in the way," Bert complained, pointing at me.

Dad just looked at me with that "I'll talk to

you later" look in his eyes, then turned back to Bert.

"Have you a description of the man?" he asked Bert. Bert's description was a bit vague, and I couldn't help much (which brought another look from dad). But what can you see when you're lying on the pavement with everybody walking over you? Grown-ups again, even those who are old enough to know better, like Bert, are brilliant at getting hold of the wrong end of the stick. Why can't they treat kids like people? Blow it, I would have to sort this thing out, and as usual it would have to be done without the help of "grown-ups" getting in the way!

We were managing to get to school on time now. Anything to avoid stupid detentions. The gang met up in the yard before school and we chatted over things. I was sometimes mean to Lump and Chip, and really regretted it afterwards. But together with Whizzer and Raj, Sparky and Sam, they were a great bunch. Problems usually happened when I thought the gang had to be good at the things I wanted them to be good at. It was like Doug sometimes said, "When God has made somebody one sort of special person, why do you, Nick, spend so much time trying to reorganize the good work?"

"Tell that to the teachers," was my usual response, but I knew what he meant. I told everyone about what had happened at Bert's and then told them that we would have to sort it out because the grown-ups couldn't handle it. There were groans all round, but I didn't get worked up, they'd soon come round to my view on the matter — one way or another!

"Doug's in school today, isn't he?" Sparky said, changing the subject.

"Yes," Raj replied. "It's to do with that social action stuff."

"Just so long as I don't get placed with anyone like that bad-tempered old bloke Bert," I responded.

In the class Miss Nolan was waiting with Doug. It was funny seeing him there, sort of on the other side. Doug told us all about what would happen, talking all about RAG, "Reaching Across Generations". Then Miss Nolan began to announce what everybody would be doing.

"We have the names of some old people in the area," she said. "And we are to visit them, spend some time helping them, then write it all up in a diary." Every time! What is it about teachers that makes them insist you have to write about everything? I wonder if they do it!

Suddenly my name was called.

"Your partner for the project, Nick," Miss Nolan announced, I swear with a twinkle in her eye, "is Samantha!"

I blushed, I couldn't help it. I didn't go slightly pink, I went a deep purply red. I looked across at Sam. She was the same colour. I looked at Doug, who was trying not to laugh. "I'll kill him later," I thought.

The class was cheering, whistling, and falling about in hysterical laughter! It wasn't that I didn't like the idea of Sam being my partner — you know what I mean? It was the embarrassment of it all!

When Miss Nolan had finally calmed everybody down, worse news was to follow.

"You two," continued Miss Nolan, "will be going to see a Mr Herbert Stokes of 27 Windmill Street."

The dreaded Bert!

I looked at Doug in absolute disgust. He just smiled back, the rat.

That first meeting with Bert was dreadful. It was everything I had expected and more!

It took Sam a long time to get me there in the first place. But I knew we had to go through with it, so eventually I found myself outside Bert's front door, forcing my hand towards the bell.

I pressed once and waited. There was no response.

"Great," I said to Sam. "No one in, let's go."

"Hang on," Sam replied. "Try again."

I pressed the bell again. Then played a tune on it, several times, until Sam stopped me.

"Who's that?" came a voice from the other side of the door. "I don't want anything, and if you don't go away I'll call the police."

"We're from the school, Mr Stokes," Sam called through the door. "To do with the helping project."

"Oh," we heard.

Then we heard bolts being slipped; the door was unlocked and opened slightly. Bert looked at Sam, then looked at me and his face dropped.

"Oh no," he said. The feeling was mutual.

"I suppose you had better come in," he muttered.

When we reached his kitchen he sat down and said, "Why did it have to be you?" I wanted to reply, but Sam was treading on my toes. I got her message!

We asked him if there was anything that he needed doing, and he suggested things like fetching shopping, cleaning up the back yard, cleaning out the kitchen cupboards.

Grief, who did he think we were, slaves?

Sam wrote everything down and kept asking him things.

I didn't say anything.

There was a sort of prickliness between me and Bert.

But Sam really got Bert talking — about how he used to be in the Salvation Army when he was younger, but then went away to war and never went back to it afterwards.

Then he went a bit upset, like old people sometimes do when they talk about the past. He told Sam that she was getting "nosey". She didn't mind, but I thought that was terrible. I felt sorry for him, but that didn't excuse him from being rude. He was old enough to know better.

As we made to go, I muttered to Sam, "Ungrateful old so-and-so."

She just whispered back to shut up.

We were on the way out when he called to us. "Er, you will be coming back won't you," he said, "to do those jobs?"

"Only if I have to," I muttered to Sam. She kicked me. Hard!

"Yes of course," I called back to him.

Down the road I turned on Sam. "Why did you kick me so hard?" I complained.

"Because sometimes, Nick, your mouth works a lot faster than your brain," she replied.

I didn't reply. I'd heard it before.

"Don't you realize that he's a very lonely old bloke?" she went on. "And that makes him a bit grumpy sometimes."

"Oh," I replied. The penny dropped! Aren't I thick?

6
Making a Splash

One of the best events of the autumn school term was the swimming gala.

I didn't think Mr Pick, our new PE teacher, could possibly mess that up, but he tried!

As many people as possible were allowed to enter the qualifying rounds, and then the finals were held on "gala night" in the school pool. This term there was a record number of entries because the early rounds took place during PE lessons and it meant getting away from the dreaded Mr Pick and his lethal training circuits.

As well as myself, Sparky, Sam, Whizzer, and Raj were in the finals. The amazing thing was that Lump made it as well — in the diving. I think he put so much effort into it to avoid another dreadful scene with "Pick". He trained like a lunatic, and was becoming quite good, provided he met the water just right. If he was slightly off target the result was spectacular.

On the night of the gala we arrived together. Chip and Mo were going to cheer us on. Outside we saw Ram and his bunch, and the usual arguments started about who was going to do best. We weren't fighting or doing anything particularly bad, just speaking fairly loudly about how well we would do.

Mr Pick didn't have the same view! He came storming out of the entrance to the pool, demanding to know what all the noise was about.

"I'm just about sick of you lot," he screamed, going right over the top. "Always in to bother of some kind. You're just typical of the grotty kids that live in this grotty area. Now get in there before I disqualify you."

I was just about to answer him back when Miss Nolan arrived and pushed us inside. "Come on, you've got more important things to be doing," she said, and gave Mr Pick a funny look.

Whizzer did well in the backstroke and won his race, and Raj had a fantastic race with one of Ram's pals, just beating him in the butterfly. I thought that was amazing because that stroke completely beats me. Whenever I try to do it I finish up a tangle of arms and legs, sinking rapidly to the bottom.

Sparky was good at everything, so he swam in the medley race, where you had to do a length each of four different strokes. He managed to come third against boys who were older than him.

Sam, of course, won her race. She was brilliant.

Poor Lump! He was trying so very hard. Too hard!

His first dive was quite good, and he was in second position.

A miracle!

Everybody stood around the pool to watch.

He set himself up for his second dive, determined to do something special.

Have you ever thrown a big rock in to a pond and seen the result? I remember watching a film once called "Krakatoa, East of Java" when there was this fantastic tidal wave which drowned hundreds of people. Lump's dive reminded me of that. He tried to do some sort of somersault and finished half way round as he approached the water.

SPLAT!!

The sound must have been heard miles away. There was a moment of silence as the water gathered its power, then WHOOSH!! Water drenched everybody, including the headmaster who looked like a drowned rat.

It was also good to see Mr Pick looking messed up. He usually looked so neat and tidy; now water dripped both from him and his wretched clipboard.

Needless to say, Lump came last. But he got a medal from me for the best performance.

For most of the evening Ram had been very quiet. I thought it was because his lot hadn't been doing too well. He was up against me in the freestyle race later on and must have been busy warming up, or so I thought!

He had other plans!

I got a message to report to Mr Pick at the poolside. As I got near to where he was standing, organizing the next race, I was stopped by Ram.

"What do you want?" I demanded.

"I was just going to wish you good luck," he replied holding out his hand.

I know, I should have smelled a rat!

"I don't need luck," I replied, smiling, and holding out my hand.

Suddenly, I felt a sharp push from behind. It was one of Ram's gang who had crept up without me noticing. At the same time Ram yanked me forward and stuck his foot out. The result was that I shot forward out of control, straight into Mr Pick!

I stopped and he flew backwards in to the pool to the cheers of every child in the place.

His clipboard landed in the middle and sank gracefully to the bottom.

He wasn't half cross. Mr Pick erupted from the water like a volcano, but he looked so silly he couldn't make too much fuss, and the papers from his clipboard surfaced and floated all around him.

"You're disqualified," was all he said through gritted teeth, as he grabbed for his soggy bits of paper.

There was no point in protesting that Ram caused it. He was nowhere to be seen.

"I'll see you tomorrow," Pick muttered as he passed me on the way to the changing rooms.

It really made me fed up. I had waited all this

time to swim, and now I was disqualified, and through no fault of my own. There was no point making a fuss, but if I could have got hold of Ram I would have done something nasty to him. This was too much!

When I did see Ram he was too far away, and too well protected by his mates. He just smirked wickedly at me. There was no need to say anything. He had won this one — this one — but there would be another time!

I got changed and left the pool feeling sad and angry, both with myself and with everyone else. As usual, things around me were going wrong, and as far as I was concerned it was not my fault! There didn't seem much point in doing the right thing every time. It didn't seem to make much difference in the end!

Eventually I found myself outside the club hut. There was a light on inside, so I went in.

Doug was there sorting some cupboards out. He was really fantastic in the amount of time he gave up for us all, but I wasn't in any mood to be grateful. I threw myself in to one of the old easy chairs.

"I see," Doug said. "Want to talk?"

I didn't reply, so Doug got on with the cupboards.

"It's not fair!" I suddenly blurted out.

Now he could have said that he'd heard all this before, but he didn't. Instead, he said, "You'd better tell me what happened."

So I told him, and while I was at it mentioned

him "showing me up" in the classroom with Sam, and one or two other things as well.

There was a silence.

I carried on. "I suupose you're going to tell me that life isn't fair. And you're going to say that as a Christian I should be learning to look at things differently. Then you're going to talk all about what Jesus would have done, and finally how God forgives us our mistakes."

It went quiet again. I was thinking about what I had said.

"OK," I went on. "I'll go and walk the dog and sort this out." Walking Wally helped me think; he didn't answer back when I moaned at him.

"Bye," Doug said as I walked out of the door. "Oh, and don't forget the meeting tomorrow night."

I had, and so had Sam, because we had arranged to see Bert.

Back home I picked up Wally, who was always keen to go for a walk, and set off to "have a think". I also asked Mo to pop in to see Bert on her way home from school the next day and tell him we couldn't make it but would call the following night. It wasn't a problem because it was on her route.

Wally and I set off towards the park.

He was a daft animal who never hurt anybody. Well that's not totally true. He was brilliant at sorting people out, and could spot a "baddie" a mile off. Anyone he judged to be bad got the

Wally treatment which usually resulted in badly damaged ankles.

My dad said he would have been a brilliant police dog if he had been a different size and shape. He reckoned Wally was made by a committee using all the bits left over from other dogs, and no two bits matched! But I liked him just the weird shape he was!

We walked, and I took the chance to have one of my little chats with God, sorting a few things out! It's great. You don't have to be in church to pray. I wasn't really thinking about where I was going, just wandering through the park with Wally sniffing about here and there.

Suddenly the lead yanked out of my hand.

We were walking past a scruffy-looking bloke who was standing just off the path. Wally snapped at the man's heels, causing him to start leaping about.

I was going to say how sorry I was, but the man started kicking out at Wally and really hurt him. This made Wally really mad.

"Get this stupid dog off me," the man yelled at me.

"Stop kicking him," I screamed back. I had hold of the lead again and was trying like mad to pull Wally off. Gradually I pulled him away, but then the bloke landed a nasty kick to Wally's side.

"Hey," I yelled. "You do that again and I'll get my dad. He's a policeman."

With that the man turned on his heels and

raced off. I was too busy helping Wally to chase him, but as I sat rubbing Wally's side, I had a funny feeling that I'd met that bloke before.

I kept thinking about it as I carried poor Wally home.

7
Taking a Short Cut

I felt a lot better at school the next day. In spite of the way that man had treated Wally, who soon recovered, the time walking and thinking had helped. I hoped that the effects would last!

Even the taunting by Ram and his mates was OK. For once I could handle it, much to everybody's surprise.

Ram kept going on and on, but even he eventually realized he wasn't getting anywhere and gave up.

I had to report to Mr Pick first thing, and even that worked out right. He was pretty unpleasant about it but that was all.

"I had a word with your form teacher, Miss Nolan, who says that she saw what happened and was sure that it wasn't your fault," he said.

"I'm really sorry you got wet," was my reply, not sure if I really meant it and thinking at the same time how fantastic Miss Nolan was. She had a voice like a foghorn, but was as soft as a jelly inside.

Thankfully Mr Pick didn't ask me who was responsible because I hated "telling" on people, even enemies. Neither did he apologize for getting me thrown out of the competition. But I didn't push it because we had him for games later that day, and I didn't want to set myself up for anything rotten he might plan. You know what teachers can be like!

All day, everybody was talking in class about Pick and what we might face now the swimming gala was over. Of all the horrible things we could think of, none of us dreamed of the foul thing he sorted out for us.

The last teacher in charge of PE was a reasonable sort of bloke who gave us different sports to try out. We also did sport with the girls, which I liked because Sam and some of her friends were far better than most of the boys in the class.

This nut had physical fitness on the brain. I bet if you split his head open it would be full of muscle with not a brain cell in sight.

"Right," he ordered as we all trooped out of the changing rooms. "I have a special treat for you today. Girls, you will be with Miss Kelly for something a little easier, er, netball or something."

I could see Sam beginning to go red. Miss Kelly didn't look too pleased either. He was a right "male chauvinist pig"!

The girls trooped off looking as if they would like to lynch our celebrated Head of the PE department.

"Well my fine friends," he began.

He was no friend of mine!

"I thought that you might like to have a little jog today," he went on.

That wasn't too bad. I quite liked the cross-country course, it was a fairly gentle jog around the park, and you could stop off for a go on the swings.

Then the bombshell!

"I looked at the course that my predecessor devised," Pick went on with an evil glint in his eye, "and decided it was far below the capabilities of the tremendous bunch of athletes that there is in this school. You will be the first to try out a new, improved little run."

He almost smiled, but none of the lads in my class did. Some looked decidedly worried!

"I have negotiated," he continued, "with the people who own the land around the reservoir at the back of our sports field, and have marked out a route for you to run — twice!"

Even I felt a bit worried about that. Langley Res. was a wicked place, all muddy paths, really hard running, and it was miles round!

We moved over to the edge of the field to start. There was a new gate that none of us had noticed before.

Ram and his pals were chatting away to each other. I wondered what they were planning!

"Now don't worry," Mr Pick added. "It's quite easy, you just follow the main path round the reservoir. Do not take the short cut over the stream! Now GO!"

Ram and his pals set off at a ridiculous pace. What were they up to?

I could have kept up, but stayed with the rest of the gang instead. We ran out of school at the back, across a road, and started along the path. We could see Ram, but he was a long way ahead.

I looked back. Thankfully Pick didn't seem to be following, but I didn't trust that guy!

Sparky, Whizzer, Raj, Lump, Chip and myself ran together. The rest of us were going to make sure Lump and Chip got round.

Chip was, as usual, dressed for the part in all the correct gear provided by his teacher dad. Poor thing, fancy having a dad who is a teacher! It must be like for ever being at school, no break. No wonder he was a nervous wreck.

Lump was in his usual gear. Old shorts and top that his dad must have owned. They were far too big for him, and his shorts tended to fall down every time he started running hard, which wasn't often! He was clutching them now as he struggled along. His fat legs were thumping along, getting redder and redder, nearly as red as his face.

We were well on the way round in the first circuit when Raj suddenly noticed something. "Hey, where's Ram's lot?" he asked. "They're not up ahead."

Sure enough, they had disappeared from view. But I knew where they were. They had taken the short cut which led over a stream that fed the reservoir. I told the gang and suggested that we should take the same route. Pick wasn't behind us, and it would really help Chip and Lump.

Sparky and Raj insisted on running all the way round the course, which I thought was daft. But I didn't make a fuss, it was up to them!

Chip and Lump thought the short cut was a great idea. So did Whizzer, who was a good runner but hated long races.

Raj and Sparky carried on and we four took the short cut. There was no sign of Ram and his gang, but they must have gone this way. We reached the stream and Lump started across the rickety stones that provided a dry route across in good weather. The stream was getting fuller as autumn progressed and had just reached the top of the stones, but you could still get across if you were careful.

Lump was very careful, but when he had got halfway across, clutching his baggy shorts, Ram and his mates popped up from the bushes on the opposite side and started throwing boulders in the water around Lump.

There was nothing we could do, and Lump soon found himself sitting in the very cold water. He did look unhappy!

We yelled at Ram's lot and threw things at them, but they just pulled faces and ran off.

When Lump stood up, the inevitable happened, he left his shorts behind. His face went even redder as he quickly covered his confusion!

By the time we had squeezed Lump dry and

made it back on to the main path, Ram's lot, and Sparky and Raj were well away. In fact, we were at the back of the whole class. There was nothing for it but to go on. We made it once round, dragging along a very wet and miserable Lump.

Mr Pick was nowhere to be seen!

The second circuit was going to be hard. At the place where the short cut went towards the stream, Lump flatly refused to take it a second time, so we carried on the long way round. We reached the place where the short cut came out, but Ram was nowhere in sight.

The last bit was agony for Lump and Chip. They hated it, but we got them round. At the finish there was no Mr Pick. Sparky and Raj were waiting and said that they had seen him near where the short cut came out.

Ram was still nowhere to be seen. What had happened?

Then Mr Pick arrived, running the wrong way round the course. He looked at Lump. "Why are you so wet boy?" he asked.

"Oh, he sweats a lot," I said, butting in quickly, then changing the subject. "Have you seen Ram and his mates, sir? They were in front of us but haven't finished."

"They'll be a little late," he replied with a wicked smile. "They've discovered that taking short cuts isn't a good idea."

We all looked at each other. So, old Pick had caught them and made them go the long way round.

Eventually they arrived, looking dreadful. For the first time Ram's gang was not happy with him, not happy at all! We cheered them in, between laughing our sweaty socks off!

Pick reckoned we were all useless and ordered us to go to shower.

In the changing rooms for once Ram wasn't getting at me. He had a bigger target, Mr Pick. We actually found ourselves agreeing for once. Could this be the end of the Ram-Nick wars? I doubted it!

Pick didn't have a good word for anybody. Something would have to be done about him though; we were all in agreement about that!

After school we were making our weary way home, with Sam telling us how she had "mashed" everybody at netball and would take us all on at cross country given half the chance, when Mo came running up all in a panic.

"I thought I asked you to see Bert and tell him we couldn't make it?" I demanded.

"I tried to," she replied breathlessly. "But I couldn't make him hear, and when I looked through the window I saw him lying on the floor."

"What!" I exclaimed. "Come on gang!"

We stretched our tired legs and ran off to Bert's house. Sure enough, through the window I could see Bert lying on the ground.

Raj ran off to call the police, while I smashed a window-pane in the door to open it from the inside. When we got to Bert he was beginning to come round and we helped him to a chair.

"My money, he got my money," he groaned.

Sparky got him a glass of water, and then my dad screeched up in his police car.

Bert told Dad that this bloke was waiting for him when he got back from the post office with his pension. When Bert opened the door, he was pushed from behind to the ground, and his pension money was taken. From the description, it was the same man as before, and he sounded a bit like the bloke I'd met in the park.

The ambulance came and took Bert to hospital for a check-up.

My dad said that it was getting worrying. The man robbing these old people was getting more dangerous. He didn't seem interested in my vague description of the man in the park. He thought Wally was daft anyway. But I was sure there was some sort of connection.

Nick and Co. would definitely have to do something about all this.

8

Paint Work

Thankfully, we had reached the weekend.

No more Pick!

No more school for two days!

Great!!

Saturday morning saw all of us cycling along to the club hut by the church. I was filling the gang in with details about the mystery man who was giving all the old folks trouble. Telling them all my theories behind what happened to Bert!

"I think this is definitely a case for us as the supreme detectives in the area," I announced to everybody.

"Not again," whined Chip. "You're always getting us in to things that mean bother."

"Oh, come on," I complained. "Look at all the excitement we've had. First there was tracking down the car thieves and the sit-in at the club hut which got us our new building. Then there was the great sheep-stealing escapade, when single-handed we sorted out that trouble in Tidesbourne."

"Regular little Robin Hood, aren't you?" Lump moaned.

Honestly, some people aren't half ungrateful for all the — excitement — I get them.

"I can't help feeling that most things would have sorted themselves out anyway, without our help," Sparky added.

"No way," I complained, nearly falling off my bike.

This wasn't at all fair. Just because there had been a few minor scrapes along the way . . . I brought the subject back to Bert.

"Look. I'm not going to sit by while that poor bloke and his mates suffer," I went on.

"That's not what you said the other day," Sam butted in. "You said that helping Bert was the last thing you wanted to do!"

I was getting fed up with this conversation and my rebellious friends! But suddenly my mind was taken on to other things.

We came across Ram!

I had thought that he was beginning to change his ways. Some hope!

Ram's lot were looking particularly evil. They refused to move over and both our sets of bikes came to a stop in the road facing each other.

"Get out the way," I demanded.

"You get out the way," was Ram's response.

Well, I certainly wasn't going to let him have the last word. "Why don't you shift those heaps of junk and let the experts through?" I went on.

"We'll see who has the heap of junk on race

day," was Ram's reply, as he aimed a kick at Chip's bike which was alongside mine.

The two sets of bikes mixed up as, with various challenges and kicks from Ram's lot, everybody passed each other. All except Ram and me that is. We both stood our ground, front wheels pushed against each other.

I think that we would be there to this day if Doug hadn't arrived in his old van and hooted his horn at us to get out of the way and let him past. By the time we had dragged our bikes clear and sorted things out, the only thing left to do was just to threaten each other!

"Just you wait till race day," I said as we parted.

"You won't have to wait that long," he replied with a wicked grin.

What did he mean?

We cycled on towards the club hut, and arrived to see Doug standing outside, shaking his head.

"What's up?" I asked as I screeched to a halt alongside him, closely followed by the rest of the gang.

"Look," he replied, pointing his finger.

The side of the hut was covered in graffiti, in all sorts of colours. I couldn't repeat what was written about all of us, but I certainly knew who had done it!

I flipped.

"That rat. That toad, Ram!" I screamed. "I'll kill him." I threw down my bike and paced about in a fury.

"Where are the paint brushes?" sighed Sparky.

"Paint brushes, paint brushes!" I fumed. "We've only just finished painting the thing. I think we should go out and get that pig Ram and make *him* paint the blinking thing."

"They're in the cupboard, Sparky," Doug said. "I'll go and get them. You fetch the paint from around the back."

"Isn't anybody listening to me?" I demanded.

"Oh, we can hear you all right," Sam replied. "I would think most of the street can hear you."

"Well," I went on.

"Well?" Sam replied.

There was a long silence.

"Look," Sparky eventually said. "You can choose between the fist or the paintbrush, but while you're making your mind up, we're all going to clean this mess up."

I looked round at everybody and the "red mist" in front of my eyes began to clear. After all, I had no proof that Ram had done it, and there was no way that I would have got him back here without a bloodbath, with a considerable amount of my blood!

I stood around kicking some stones while the paint and brushes were collected.

Ungratefully I grabbed a brush and a tin of paint from Sparky and went off to the far end of the hut on my own. I thrust the brush into the pot and banged it on the hut wall.

Everybody got on with the job and didn't say much. It was all very tense. I worked my way along, slapping the paint on the wall, taking out my anger on it, not thinking of anything except the stupid paint and stupid Ram.

I didn't notice the paint tin being used by Whizzer.

He didn't notice me, because as usual he was listening to his Walkman, painting along to the rhythm of his favourite music.

Suddenly I kicked the paint tin and it sprayed all over. I naturally blamed Whizzer and turned round to push him. In doing so, I put my foot in the spilt paint. Did you know that spilt paint is very slippy? It is!

My feet shot from under me and I sat down hard in the middle of the mess. In my hand I had the paintbrush and my tin of paint. As I jolted to the ground, my paint and brush shot from my grasp straight up in the air, then down again to land neatly on top of my head, raising a lump, and depositing paint all over my face, in my hair, down my neck, everywhere!

The others fell about laughing.

Lump laughed so much he tripped on one end of the plank he was standing by, shooting his tin of paint into the air, travelling through a graceful arc, and landing — yes, you've guessed it — right in my lap.

Everybody laughed so much they were nearly sick.

I didn't! I suddenly thought of what Mum and Dad would say. Although these were old clothes, they'd kill me!

The laughter stopped. They could see I wasn't amused.

"You better come inside with me, Nick," Doug said, "And we'll clean you up. There are some old clothes you can put on. Sparky, you see to the rest of the painting."

I followed Doug and we went through the long slow process of cleaning up.

It was a right mess, and hadn't made me any better tempered.

"Some friends I've got," I complained.

"Come on, Nick," Doug replied. "Your friends are great. Don't tell me you wouldn't have laughed if it had been somebody else."

I didn't reply.

"Friends are very important — don't take yours for granted. You've got some great ones," he went on.

I winced. I could feel a sermon coming on.

"Your friends have stuck with you through thick and thin," he continued. "They don't let you down, even when you get them into bother, get angry, or generally cause them a lot of hassle. You've also got another friend, you know!"

"You're not talking about Ram are you?" I responded suspiciously.

"Of course not," he replied.

"Oh, you mean Jesus," I said.

I'd known what he meant all the time.

"Yes," he continued. "And good friends like yours are always there to listen when things don't go right."

It was true. I remembered that time in the park. Doug went outside to help clear up, and I had a little chat with God while I was left on my own.

By the time the gang came in I had sorted myself out and we had a good time planning how we would win the cycle race. Then Doug came home with me, which was great. "Mums find it hard to get cross with sons when the local curate brings them home to explain" is a good piece of advice to anyone daft enough to sit in a pot of paint.

That was a quick answer to my prayer!

9

Surprises all Round

Sunday passed by reasonably well. On Sunday nights we went back to Doug's house for some singing and supper. I really enjoyed those times. They were a chance to charge yourself up for the week ahead.

I was really going to need it this week!

On the Monday we were going on a museum trip.

Boring, boring. Yawn, yawn!

Miss Nolan said it would be good because they were putting on a special science and technology display that was travelling round the country.

Sounded like teacher talk to me, you know what I mean?

The worst thing was having to meet Ram and not punch him in the face.

Mum had made my favourite sandwiches for school trips: cream cheese and piccalilly. It turned everybody else's stomachs, but I loved it, especially when it was put on in stripes.

As soon as we were in school Ram started

making comments about the nice new paint on the club hut wall. He just went on and on and on. It seemed to me he was trying desperately hard to impress his gang after that trouble in the cross-country.

Getting on the bus was as chaotic as ever. Everybody fought to be at the front of the queue so that they could grab the back seat on the bus.

I had a hunch that Miss Nolan would pull a "teacher's trick", and held back with the rest of the gang. No teacher was going to outsmart me. My guess was right! When she eventually managed to get everybody in some sort of line, she turned us all round and the back became the front.

We made it to the back seat, much to Ram's disgust because his lot had bullied their way to the front of the queue. They were forced to sit somewhere in the middle of the bus on the only remaining seats.

We jeered as they got on last.

Of course, in the end it only made things worse. Ram got in a mood and started making comments again. I tried to ignore him by spending the time waving and giving the thumbs-up sign to motorists behind us on the bus, but it was difficult — the comments were like a constantly dripping tap.

I didn't get mad though. I was trying really hard.

The rest of the gang kept me busy with jokes, trying to keep the nagging Ram behind a wall of noise. His voice still kept coming through but, for the first time really, I *wasn't* getting mad. I felt a bit sorry for Ram. I kept thinking how snarled up he must be inside to be like that all the time. Even when the gang started throwing half sucked sweets and "chewed" gum at me, I managed to stay calm.

Eventually we got to the museum, the same boring old museum I had visited before on school trips. Why do teachers think kids "love" museums?

I can't even think why so many teachers like them!

But when we got inside there was an amazing surprise. In four of the main rooms all the exhibits had been cleared out and there were loads of scientific gadgets and television screens. And we were allowed to touch and play with them.

Fantastic. No grumpy old museum attendants for ever telling us off.

Before we were allowed loose we had to go through the usual ritual of "the talk". First some bloke went on about science and mechanics. Only Chip listened, the rest of us were desperate to get going. If only adults realized it has to be the action first. Then we might listen to the talk!

Finally we were told to "not do anything stupid" by Miss Nolan.

As if we would!

Then we rushed in to action. There were buttons to press, gadgets to work, machines to try, videos to watch, it was fantastic.

Sparky, Sam and I went straight to a corner that was all about space. We sat in a mock-up of a space buggy and watched a video about the moon. You could imagine you were actually driving along on the moon's surface because the buggy moved and jumped about in time with the video.

I worked the steering wheel which was a bit wobbly. I think it was cracked a bit, probably too many kids using it, but it didn't stop the fun.

Then there was a dark box you could step inside and watch a rocket take off while you wore headphones that gave you the sound. It was incredible.

I went in with Sam, which was a daft mistake! When we came out you should have heard the whistles and seen the winks. We both blushed so much we looked like a pair of red lollipops!

Chip had found the computers and was busy typing in all sorts of things and getting replies. He was chatting away to the bloke who gave the talk at the beginning about something that sounded like Martian to me.

Whizzer and Raj had gone to some things that tested their strength, and we went over to watch. They were running on a conveyor belt, then putting their hand on a machine that tested their heartbeat. Sparky suggested I should have put my hand on the machine when I came out of the dark box with Sam.

We both hit him!

We were having a great time. Fortunately

Ram and his mates had gone off somewhere and weren't bothering us.

We all had our sandwiches in the park outside the museum at lunch. There was time for a game of football, but none of our lot played. We didn't want any trouble with Ram's lot. Of course, they yelled and taunted us for being whimps, but it wasn't worth rising to the bait; I knew Ram was spoiling for a fight and I wasn't going to give him one. It only caused me bother in the end.

After lunch we got the other teacher ploy thrust at us.

The questionnaire! Fill in the spaces, some with drawings, some with written answers. Why do teachers try so hard to make exciting things boring?

I bet that later it would be the things I had *chosen* to do in the morning that I would remember, not the things I had been *made* to do in the afternoon. Still, that's what the game of school is all about!

I managed to get the work done, and made my way to the entrance with Sam and Sparky. Miss Nolan was there collecting things and sorting us out.

Then the man who had talked to us in the morning came storming up. He didn't look so friendly now.

"Someone," he announced, "has deliberately broken the space buggy exhibit."

We all trooped over to where it was.

Miss Nolan was looking angry and embarrassed.

The steering column of the machine had been broken off.

She turned on us. "Which one of you did this?" she demanded angrily.

Now whoever did it was not likely to say, "Please, miss, it was me." What a daft question.

Then one of Ram's gang piped in. "Please Miss, Nick Baker was on that machine a lot," the squirt whinged.

I went red again.

Everyone looked accusingly at me. It was so tempting to get worked up and lose my temper, I could feel that old bubbling up inside feeling, but I didn't. God must have been listening to me! I hadn't done anything wrong.

"Miss, it wasn't me," I said quietly and calmly.

"Huh!" muttered Ram.

What was going to happen now? Would I get "done" for something I hadn't "done"?

Then one of the attendants came out from a room. What none of us realized was that the museum was on closed-circuit television. He had seen who broke the steering column.

It was Ram!

He went red and his mouth fell open.

"I . . . I . . . I . . . ," he gasped.

Miss Nolan was furious. "What on earth did you do that for?" she bellowed. "I can't take you anywhere."

"But, Miss," Ram whined. "It just broke in my hands. I thought you wouldn't believe me so I didn't say anything."

Neither Miss Nolan, nor the man in charge of the exhibits believed him. You could tell from their faces! Ram was getting into awful trouble and I had every right to really enjoy it. After all, he and his mates were trying to get me blamed for it.

You won't believe what happened next — I can't explain it. I actually helped Ram!

"Excuse me," I butted in to the tirade against Ram.

The room fell silent.

"Actually, the machine was damaged when I tried it early this morning," I went on. "I'm not surprised it broke."

There was general amazement.

Miss Nolan was like a punctured balloon. "Well, if Nick says that, it must be true," she said to the man. "Because these two really are total enemies."

The man wasn't too happy, but he didn't argue. He just went off muttering about schoolchildren.

Ram's mouth was open so wide you could have driven a bus in it!

I didn't know whether to be pleased or not!

Miss Nolan, in a daze, decided it was time to go. She counted us up and that was when we discovered Lump was missing!

From past experience, the choice of where he might be was limited.

Sam took over. "Where are all the places you can buy food?" she asked an attendant.

We found there were only two choices: the café in the art gallery next door and the ice-cream kiosk in the park. As no one had seen him since lunch, it was a good guess that he had never made it back for the afternoon.

Sure enough, he was there, still stuffing himself with ice-cream. There was no point in getting mad, he was just a food addict. The guy needed sympathy! I don't think Miss Nolan saw it that way, but by then she was too far gone to care.

Ram had regained his composure by the time we were all on the coach. He even thanked me, which was a bit embarrassing, and the rest of his gang didn't like it either. He even insisted we had the best seats at the back.

This turned out not to be a good idea. Lump had eaten so much ice-cream that he threw up halfway home, and we had a very uncomfortable journey, trying not to be sick ourselves!

Miss Nolan was past caring, so we sorted Lump out.

Teachers have no stamina!

10
Bad News!

Ram avoided me for the next week or so.

I don't think he could make me out. I wasn't sure I could make myself out.

We hadn't heard much about the school being closed and were beginning to think that it wasn't going to happen. Then we got a shock in one of our morning assemblies.

Mr Potter came in to assembly as usual, swirling along in his black gown, like Count Dracula on his way for a swift pint of blood. He never looked very happy in the morning, which didn't seem the best way to take assembly, but today he looked gloomier than ever!

The rest of the staff looked a bit glum as well, even more than usual. Apart from Mr Pick, that is, who was looking like the cat that got the cream. Something was up!

We had our usual hymn, talk, and prayer. However, instead of the usual immediate retreat by ''Potty'' at the end, he stopped and asked us to sit quietly as he had something to announce. This was very unusual.

Potty looked sad.

"I thought that you ought to be among the first to know officially,' he announced glumly.

What was he going on about? We all looked at each other.

"As school rolls are falling, there has to be some reorganization of schools in the area," he went on. "It has been decided that this school will close from next September. You and the staff will all be transferred to nearby schools!"

There was a stunned silence.

Then, without thinking I just called out, "No!" Some older kids in the row behind took it up and started chanting, "No, no, no . . ."

The staff tried hard to stop it, but the noise just grew. It took about ten minutes for things to calm down, and you'll never guess who was blamed for it all.

That rat of a teacher, Pick, reckoned it was all my fault, and I found myself outside the Head's study yet again. This time my dad would be called, for sure. He would be steaming mad and I would get sent to my room. I could see it all happening.

Along came Potty, and I waited for the worst.

"Right, off you go," was all he said. You could have knocked me down with a feather!

"Your friend told me it wasn't you and pointed out those responsible," was all he said before I was shooed away to my class.

I tried thanking Sam, Sparky, Whizzer, Raj,

Chip, *and* Lump, but they all said they'd had nothing to do with it.

I just shook my head. Who had done it?

And then I found out. Miss Nolan told me when we got back to the classroom. It was Ram!

What do you say when someone like that does something like that?

"We're quits now," he said, shrugging his shoulders when I tried to thank him. Something was happening to Ram.

Miss Nolan got us sitting down quietly and tried to explain about our new schools, but that just set us going again.

All that day, whatever the lesson, in the school yard, at lunch-time, all anybody could talk about was the closing of the school and where we would be transferred. It was horrible. The place was a bit scruffy. Some of the kids and teachers were a real pain. But it was our school, our home. The thought of having to make new friends, in a new building that was somebody else's school, sounded terrible.

Even the teachers were very low and miserable. Nobody could get them worked up, apart from Pick that is. What a good job we didn't have him that day!

Something would have to be done. We couldn't just let the school die without a fight!

After school Sam, Sparky and I went to the club hut to meet Doug, Mo and Wally. We were planning to go to see Bert. He had been pretty badly shaken up and the hospital had kept him in for a couple of days. I still wasn't that keen on Bert, but I didn't like the thought of old people getting treated like that.

When we got to Bert's house he wasn't going to let us in. We knocked, and there was no answer.

"Hello Bert," Doug called.

"Go away," grunted Bert from inside.

"Come on Bert, it's us," I added.

"Not today, thanks," Bert called back.

"Nutty old folks," I grumbled to everybody.

"If you don't go away I'll call the police," Bert yelled from inside.

"That'll be difficult," I muttered. "He's not on the phone!"

"Oh, shut up, Nick," Sam complained. Then turning to the door she called to Bert, "Go to the window, Bert. And you can see who it is." What a good idea. Why didn't I think of that? We saw the net curtains pull back and Bert looked out. He looked very suspicious. Then we heard the sound of bolts being drawn back, and slowly the door was opened.

"I suppose you had better come in," he mumbled. He didn't look the same Bert that had helped us in the park. He was bruised all over his face, and had a limp.

In his small old-fashioned front room, he sat down and told us to do the same. "I'm sorry for sounding so funny," he said. "But you can't be too careful these days. I am very grateful for the help you gave to me when I was attacked by that man. Would you like a biscuit? They're in the tin on the sideboard."

I was about to move when I felt Sam's hand on my shoulder. "No thanks," she said. "We're all going to have our tea soon."

I just fancied a biscuit!

"Do you need anything?" Doug asked.

"No, nothing thank you very much," Bert replied respectfully. It was horrible the way old Bert had been beaten up, even though I had thought him a bit of a pain. He was in a very sad mood; there was nothing we could do to cheer him up, so we soon left. He said he was tired.

Life was going to be very busy — sorting out the school *and* finding the monster that was attacking the old folk.

On the way back to the hut Sam asked Doug what we could do to help Bert.

"He doesn't want any help," I butted in. "He said so."

"You are a Wally, Nick," Sam responded. "He's a lonely, sad, frightened old man. He's desperate for help."

I don't think I will ever understand other people. They never say what they mean. I always do — then end up in bother for it!

Doug reckoned I was just the sort of person Bert needed around, but I couldn't see it. He didn't seem to like me, but Doug said he did.

"I think he was probably like you when he was young," Doug said to me.

"You must be joking," I replied in disbelief.

"Just wait till you're Bert's age," Sam added. "I can just see you going on about children always causing trouble — buzzing their space jets around your head, and not being respectful."

I gave her a push because I couldn't think of anything to say.

The others just laughed.

"Last one to the hut's a Wally," I shouted, changing the subject. I set off at a dash, gaining a good distance before the others came after me. Everybody ran, except Doug, but I knew Lump and Chip would be complaining all the way.

I was so far in front that I had time to look round and yell back at everybody. "Can't catch me," I bellowed. "The fastest in the land. Steve Cram, eat your heart out!"

As usual I was going over the top.

As usual I was too busy showing off to look where I was going.

As usual that led to disaster!

Suddenly I crashed full speed into something soft — another innocent human being! This was becoming a habit. Only this one wasn't so innocent. It was a kid from Ram's gang.

The rest of our lot skidded to a halt, facing Ram's mates. I looked up to find Ram staring down at me. This looked like trouble, big trouble!!

"I've been looking for you," Ram said very severely. "I want a word with you!"

11

Protest Plan

I looked up at Ram.

I expected him to take advantage of the position I was in. There was a long silence, nobody knew what to say.

Ram's arm stretched out to me and I flinched, but he wasn't trying to hit me, he was reaching down to help me up.

I couldn't believe this, but in a daze I accepted the pull up to my feet. Ram was obviously struggling to say something. We stood looking at each other, as did Doug and the members of both gangs. It was really weird.

Eventually Ram spoke. "I . . . er . . . wanted to . . . er . . . say I was sorry for some of the things that have happened between us," he mumbled.

This was amazing.

He didn't go into details, and I was so dumbstruck I didn't push it. Anyway, I had done some pretty wicked things to him in the past, and I didn't want to go through all those!

"Great," I responded to his apology, which

was a pretty stupid thing to say, but it was all I could think of.

"I wondered if we might do something together about the closing of the school?" Ram went on.

"Sure," I replied.

There was another awkward silence, then Doug stepped up, thankfully, and took over.

"I have an idea," he said. "Let's have a proper meeting to chat things over, rather than standing here blocking the street."

Ram and I readily agreed. Anything to get away from this! Doug arranged for us to meet the following night at the club hut, and we went our separate ways.

The next day in school was weird, with Ram being very quiet. Miss Nolan got very confused. She was sure we were all up to something because it was so peaceful. By the end of the day she was really twitchy and nervous, shouting at us for nothing, and I mean nothing!

You can't win with teachers. They're nuts. Mind you, they were probably quite normal before they started teaching. It must be some sort of disease they catch from the chalk!

"See you tonight," Ram said as we separated at the end of school. I nodded back at him, still not quite sure if all this was real or some dreadful trick.

We all got to the club early, just in case this was a set-up.

Doug was there as well. He obviously thought it was important, because he had brought in biscuits and squash.

"Anybody would think we had the queen coming," I replied. We never get biscuits except on really special occasions, and here we had the biggest rogue in the district coming — the one who had put graffiti all over the hut walls — and Doug was pulling out all the stops.

Doug suggested we pray about the meeting.

"Trust you to think of that," I grumbled. But underneath I reckoned we really did need God to help with this one.

Doug prayed that there would be a good time, and that we might be able to patch up our differences. I thought that was asking a lot of God, but happily added my, "Amen".

After a bit I got up and had a game of pool with Raj, but I couldn't concentrate. It was really weird. We were all a bit edgy. So much so that I lost to Raj for the first time. I sat down again.

"Well, it looks like they're not turning up," I eventually said. "I thought they wouldn't. They're probably too chicken."

"Oh come on," Doug cut in. "Give them a chance. Why do you always have to think the worst?"

"I remember!" I responded.

"You forget!" Doug replied. "You forget what you were like and how impossible it seemed that you might change."

I grunted and shrugged my shoulders. What

else could I do!

"They're here!" Sparky called from the window, making me jump.

I dashed over to have a look. It was like a scene from one of those black-and-white cowboy movies that you watch on wet summer afternoons. Ram and his mob were coming down the street in a line, with Ram slightly in front.

I half expected him to stop and challenge me to, "Come outside and go for your gun!" But he didn't; he kept on coming.

I dashed back to the chairs and hurtled into one, trying to look cool, calm and collected.

There was a knock on the door, and before Doug could get there to open it, I yelled out in a bossy sort of way, "Come in." I had to make sure Ram knew who was the boss around here! Doug looked at me with a pained expression on his face.

The door opened!

"Come in, Ram." Doug welcomed our old enemy — like he was an old pal. But I guess he did the right thing to get the ice broken, because it helped Ram's gang not to feel so edgy and helped get us talking.

Over the juice and biscuits we talked about some of the awful things we had done to each other in the past. It sounded quite funny looking back, though at the time we had both got steamed up in turn.

We all soon got on to talking about the school. It seemed natural as we talked about the scrapes we had got into with the teachers, and how awful or great some of them were. We all thought Miss Nolan was all right and Mr Pick was the pits. But we all agreed that it was *our* school and we didn't want to go anywhere else!

"I've played football at all the schools in the neighbourhood," Whizzer commented. "And they were all awful." For Whizzer to speak much was a miracle, and we all agreed with his view on the other schools.

"Anyway," I added. "I don't really care about other schools, this is ours and I for one am not going to let anybody take it away without a fight."

Everybody cheered in agreement!

"What are we going to do about it, then?" Ram asked.

I couldn't believe this. The thought of Ram's lot and our gang working together on anything was "out of sight", and "truly amazing".

"I think," Ram went on, "that what is needed is some sort of action campaign."

"What about a protest march?" Raj suggested.

That went down like a lead balloon. We all remembered the last time — when we were protesting about the youth club being knocked down, and Ram's lot created havoc.

The idea of petitions and a sit-in was mentioned and thrown out with the same speed as the march. We all remembered the chaos and the problems they had caused. Even though Ram was on our side this time, those ideas still made me nervous, and Doug was definitely not keen.

"It doesn't affect you," I responded to Doug.

"Look," Doug replied. "You know as well as I do that I will get drawn in to it, and that involves the church, so those ideas are definitely out."

Sam had a better idea.

"What about a proper poster campaign?" she said. "And we could write to the local papers. After the time we saved the youth club and caught those car thieves, and then that business with sheep stealing, people are bound to listen to us."

"Yes," Sparky went on. "We could also contact the local radio station. They could interview us. Hey, and we could write to our local Member of Parliament, he'd help, you know, the one who got in on the act when we opened our new club hut."

These were great ideas. Even Doug thought so.

"What about a logo?" Chip butted in. "We've got to have a logo."

There was a silence while everybody thought. You could hear the brain cells churning, or perhaps it was Lump's sweet wrappers!

"I know," Sam said. "SOS — Save Our School."

I wish I had a brain like Sam, she was so quick! It was a great idea for a logo, nobody could disagree.

Ram was getting a bit fidgety, and his gang were sitting around like lemons. They weren't exactly geniuses!

"What do you think?" I asked Ram.

"'s all right," he muttered. "But it all sounds a bit soft to me. I thought we could do something with a bit more — action!"

"Got any better ideas?" I challenged.

"Yeah," he went on. "I reckon we should go and stand outside Old Bolton's shop with banners, chanting and all that, and make it difficult for his customers to get in. That would stir things up a bit. He's the one behind it all."

I thought that was quite a good idea, but then Doug joined in. "You can't do that," he said. "It wouldn't work, and anyway it's against the law."

"Just a minute," Ram butted in. "It was my idea, and I think it is a good one. Nick doesn't have to come along, but the others can."

Doug was still very much against the idea.

"Look," Ram went on, getting mad. "This is serious, and pussyfooting around isn't going to do anything. You lot have all gone soft. Come on, gang. This place isn't for us. We'll have to do something on our own."

He got up, followed by his mates, and walked out. They kicked a few chairs to show how tough they were, and slammed the door for good measure.

There was another silence.

"They've got no patience have they?" I said. "I just can't stand people that lose their temper so quickly."

There were groans all round, and I was bombarded with cushions. I can't think why!

12

Wally to the Rescue

Things were very quiet in school. Nearly everybody was fed up with the thought of the school closing, and that put a damper on everything. There wasn't even much bad behaviour.

Letters went out to all our parents, telling them about the closure, and inviting them to a meeting. My dad had to get special time off work to go. He went to the school when he was a boy, and so did his pal, Sam's and Sparky's dad. Our mums had been pupils there, too, so it was a real family outing when they all got ready to go together.

We were annoyed that children were not invited. It was our school, why shouldn't we go?

Adults are always like that. Nobody thinks that we have anything to say. Nobody listens. They just argue loudly and then say, "What do you know, you're only a child?" Ever heard that?

We all went along and stood outside the school hall.

Sparky gave me a leg-up so that I could listen

in to what was happening. It was typical of adults. First, Mr Bolton spoke.

All the parents sat there listening. Why weren't they standing up and shouting!

Then some guy who said he was chairman of the PTA got up and said that the parents thought that was all a load of rubbish, but in a polite sort of way. This time there was loads of clapping at the end of every sentence.

Then Bolton spoke again, totally ignoring what the PTA guy had said.

This was useless and getting nowhere.

"What's happening? What's happening?" the kids were asking.

"Not a lot," was my reply.

I got down and leaned against a wall.

Ram had turned up with his pals, and he was in no mood to keep quiet, He started a chant.

"Leave our school alone! Leave our school alone!" he started. Then he picked up on Sam's idea: "SOS. Save our school! SOS. Save our school!"

The chant started quietly, then the gang all joined in. It got noisier and noisier as the chanting grew to a shout, and more kids joined in. It must have been deafening in the hall.

Mr Pick came out to try to shut us up, but however loud he shouted we just shouted louder.

I climbed back up to see what was happening in the hall. It seemed as chaotic inside as outside and eventually the parents stormed out.

Dad insisted that I came home, even though I wanted to stay and enjoy the fun, but I was determined that this wouldn't be the end of it. Nick Baker would have to do what the grown-ups didn't seem able to manage. I asked Dad if I could go to the club hut to see my mates.

"OK," he replied. "But no bother. Keep your nose out of things."

I didn't answer. I didn't want to lie!

It was time for Wally's walk and Mo was already at the hut, so I took him along with me.

He was a daft dog, with one ear bigger than the other, a permanent silly smile on his face, a fat belly, and skinny legs. A real mongrel! We had tried to train him, but he was a bit stupid and kept forgetting what he was supposed to do! He also couldn't walk in a straight line; I don't know why!

Anyway, I was walking along with Wally. Well, it wasn't really walking. He was dragging me along in a sort of zig-zag — when I heard a shout. A man rushed out of a house followed by an old lady shouting, "Help, help."

Straight away I knew it was the con-man again. The bloke rushed off down the street.

"Let's get him Wally," I yelled. Nick Baker, ace detective on the spot again, helped by his savage hound.

I could see the headlines.

We raced after him. Well, I raced after the bloke; Wally just raced. He thought it was a game and didn't realize we were actually chasing somebody. I kept yelling, "Get him Wally." But it had no effect on the stupid dog. Twice I was catching up on the thief when Wally pulled me off in another direction, and I had to stop and drag him back on the track.

We were heading in the general direction of the park. I hadn't really thought what I would do if I caught up with the guy. He looked a bit too big for me and Wally to handle. Wally would probably go up to him and hold out a paw to shake, the dumb animal.

The man turned in to the entrance to the park, and we followed. Wally thought this was great, a play in the park! Then came trouble.

There was nobody about in the park, and all of a sudden the man stopped, turned, and faced me. I skidded to a stop, holding hard on to Wally's lead.

"Get lost, kid, before I thump you," the man snarled.

For once I was lost for words. What do you do?

Then Wally took the matter out of my hands. Now, he is a bit thick, and slow on the uptake, and he may not have understood the words, but when he saw that bloke's face he certainly got the picture. He also suddenly recognized him as the same man that had kicked him before. The low growl started at the back of his throat and grew till his teeth were bared. Then, quite suddenly, the lead slipped out of my hands and he went for the thief. He made a grab at the man's legs and got a mouthful of trouser.

"Get off, get off, you stupid dog," he yelled. Then with his other leg he gave Wally a vicious kick, and then another that sent Wally spinning away, howling.

The man ran off, and I ran to Wally's side. The poor dog just lay there whining. He didn't move.

"Oh Wally, what have you done?' I groaned.

I forgot everything else, as I looked down on my injured pal. This time the man really had hurt him. I didn't want to cry, but it was difficult not to.

"God, please make Wally better." I prayed harder than I had prayed for anything before.

Gently I picked Wally up and carried him home. All the way I talked softly to him, and he whined back.

Mum and Mo were really upset when I got home. Mum rang the police station to ask Dad what to do, but he was out on a job, probably seeing the old lady who had been robbed.

We decided to carry Wally round to the vet near church. Wally hated vets, and as soon as we turned in to the gate at the vet's he started whining louder. That gateway meant pain to Wally and he didn't want to go. A bit like me and the dentist's!

We laid him out on the vet's table and he looked up at us with his pathetic eyes. After a careful examination, the vet said that she would have to keep Wally in because he might have internal injuries.

Wally whined even louder when he realized he was going to be left behind. He had a look on his face that seemed to say, "I go and rescue you, and this is the way you treat me. Some friend you are!"

We were all a bit choked up, leaving Wally, and walked home very quietly.

When we got there Dad was waiting. "What's up?" he asked. "Why did you ring the station?"

Mum told him about Wally being injured.

"Will he be all right?" Dad went on.

"We won't know till tomorrow," was the reply from Mum.

"How did it happen?" he continued.

So I told him all about chasing the man, and then him turning on us and Wally getting kicked.

"So you were the boy that gave chase," Dad said. "The old lady mentioned it in her statement. Now, lad, I want you to try and give me a description of the man."

I tried to help, but all I could think of was Wally lying on that table whining. I just couldn't think straight. Dad was very patient, because he could see I was upset, and eventually he gave up. I would have to go down to the station to look at some photographs some time, but not until this thing with Wally was sorted.

That night I just couldn't settle. I couldn't watch TV, so I went to bed early, but then I couldn't sleep. Thank goodness I had someone

special to talk to and share my worries with —
and I knew God was listening. That didn't mean
that I knew Wally would be all right. But I wasn't
alone, somebody was sharing my worries with
me. Someone else was in charge.

13

"Happy Birthday"

The following day at school was agony. Before school there had been no phone call from the vet, so Wally couldn't be dead, could he? I hurtled home after school, and there still hadn't been a phone call. As soon as Mo got home, Mum, Mo and I went round to the vet's.

"How's Wally?" I demanded, as soon as the vet's head popped round the door.

"You'd better come in and see," she replied.

Mum, Mo and I followed the vet into her surgery. Wally wasn't there.

"I won't be a minute," she said, and went out of another door.

I looked at Mum and Mo, feeling sick inside. We all looked worried.

Suddenly there was a scratching outside, the door crashed open, and Wally steamed in, dragging the vet behind him. It was an absolute miracle! Wally was all right.

When he saw us he went berserk. He wagged his tail so much that it was thumping against the furniture and knocking things over. Mo and I got such a licking as we knelt down to greet him.

"There was no serious damage," the vet said over the uproar. "But he is still very sore around his middle, so he must be stopped from racing around for a while."

"If that's possible," Mum replied.

"I think you'll find the dog himself will want to stay quiet until it gets less painful," the vet responded. I wasn't so sure, knowing my crazy pet. But he did yelp when I tried to give him a hug.

After Mum had paid the bill, which made her gasp, we took Wally home.

"Your dad's going to be a bit upset when he sees the size of this bill," Mum said as we got back home. "It's a good job he's already got your birthday present."

In all the worry over Wally, I'd forgotten it was my birthday the following day. I hoped Dad wouldn't be too worked up over the bill. Wally couldn't help it, he was only trying to protect me.

Dad mumbled, groaned and complained like dads do when they talk about money, trying to make you feel guilty. You know the line, "I go out and earn it; you go out and spend it." But he soon got over it. I think he had been worried about Wally but didn't want to show it!

I went down to the hut that night, to tell them how Wally was, but everybody was acting very strangely. When I got to the hut and opened the door, everything went silent. I thought it was because they were worried about Wally, but all the time I was playing pool and darts, some of the gang were huddled in a corner talking, and when I went over to join in they stopped.

How rude! I left in a huff!

All the next day everybody was funny. I got cards all right, but no presents. You can't ask for presents, but I was distinctly dischuffed when I didn't get any, not even from my own family. What was going on?

After school, Sparky suggested a bike ride, but I wasn't too keen. I was trying not to use my bike too much because it was getting old and battered, and I wanted to make it through the bike race. However, he persisted, and we rode off round the park.

I was feeling really grumpy and fed up inside, but didn't want to show it. Mum had made a really useless tea as well, just a few sandwiches, and I was hungry! What a grotty birthday. Nobody cared!

Not even the hilarious sight of Mr Pick out training the cycle team from Bolton's shop cheered me up. They were all dressed in identical cycle gear and had bikes from the shop. The team had been picked from a few goody-goodies in the school athletics squad. They were riding along in single file with Pick in the lead. He was bellowing orders and going faster, then slower. He had them lifting one hand from the handlebar, putting it back, then the other, then one foot, then the other. It did look stupid!

I started singing:

"You put your left foot in,
Your left foot out,
In, out, in, out,
Shake it all about.
You do the hokey-cokey
and you turn around,
That's what it's all about.
Oh, hokey . . ."

"Push off, Baker," Pick shouted, nearly falling over as he did so.

Sparky pulled me away before I got into real bother.

"Come on, we've got to go to the club hut," he said.

"Why?" I responded. "You didn't want to go there before."

"Er . . . Doug wants to see you," he replied. It didn't make sense, but I followed him anyway. Why not? At least someone wanted to see me on my birthday. Maybe he had a present for me! Sparky held back at the door of the hut and I, in my usual fashion, barged in. You could have knocked me down with a feather at what met me when I walked in.

"Happy Birthday!"

Everybody was there. All my mates, Mum, Dad, Mo, Grannie and Grandad who lived in a bungalow in Skegness, Doug, and even Wally. I just stood there with my mouth open, while everybody stood round laughing and puffing into those silly curly things that straighten out when you blow them.

"What . . . where . . . who . . . ?' I gasped out.

"Don't ask daft questions," Doug yelled out above the noise. "Just enjoy it."

I felt a right twit, I can tell you. I had been moaning and groaning about everybody all day and they had this planned for me all the time.

"Whose idea was it?" I demanded.

"Why, Sam's, of course," Doug replied, and winked.

I didn't know whether to blush, laugh, or change the subject, so I did all three. "What happens now?" I asked.

"We eat," Mum cut in, and so we did. There was so much food that it looked as though the table might break if it wasn't relieved of the load! Before we started, Sparky thanked God for the food. "Let's pray," he called, and everyone was quiet. "Thanks God," he went on, "for this lovely spread of food. And thank you for a good friend like Nick on his birthday."

I felt very good about my pals. They were brilliant. Some kids spend all their time trying to wind you up, or are only friends if you give them things or let them have their own way. My pals were different. They really wanted the best for each other, and most times tried to share everything they had. That's how it ought to be — like having Jesus for your friend.

The food soon began to disappear. Especially with Lump, the human vacuum cleaner, around. After fighting our way through mounds of sandwiches and crisps, we got on to the jellies.

Even Grandad liked the jellies. It was easy for him to eat them. Mind you, it was funny when his top set of false teeth dropped out into his jelly and he had to fish them out — much to Grannie's disgust.

"Oh, Charlie," she complained. "I can't take you anywhere."

Grandad gave a toothless grin and we all fell about laughing.

In his enthusiasm to get at the jelly, Lump dropped at least one bowl on the floor and had to be restrained from scooping it back into his dish to eat it. Sometimes he was disgusting.

Something was missing from this do. But I couldn't work out what, because I was too busy enjoying myself. Then I realized that I still hadn't had any presents! Before I had time to start nosing around, a cake appeared, made by Sparky and Whizzer, who were the best in the class at Domestic Science. It was better than my mum could do, and was covered in icing, with football players on the top, all in a Liverpool kit.

"Cut the cake! Cut the cake!" everyone demanded.

As I did, everyone sang "Happy Birthday", and Sam gave me a kiss. More embarrassment. There's a time and a place for everything!

All my pals gave me presents, mostly to do

with bikes. Whizzer gave me a lamp, Raj a bell, Lump a cap, and Chip some special stickers. Doug had bought me a book on cycling, and Sam and Sparky gave me some cycling clothes — shorts and a top. But there was nothing from the family!

Then it went quiet. Dad stepped forward.

"Well, Nick," he started, in a Dad sort of a voice. "The family, Grannie, Grandad, Mo, Mum and I have all clubbed together to get you this."

From behind his back he gave me a spanner! Then from behind a chair he gave me a wheel! Dad wasn't usually into jokes, so this was very strange.

I stood there looking dumb. What was it all about?

"Th . . . thank you," I responded. "It's just what I've always wanted!"

Everybody just stood there, until suddenly Mo cracked up. Then everybody fell about laughing.

"The rest's around the back," Dad added, with his funny Dad-type laugh, when he looks like the laughing policeman you see at the seaside.

I ran out of the hut and round to the back with the others following. There stood a brand new, glistening mountain bike, with the front wheel missing!

It was fantastic!

I put the wheel on and pushed it in to the hut.

"Thanks Dad," I gasped. "Thanks everyone."

At that moment I was the happiest person in the whole world. Everyone sat around for a bit while I sat amongst my presents, holding each one in turn.

When I had started thinking straight again, I spoke again. It seemed sort of the right thing to do. I thanked my mum and dad, and all my friends for the party and everything. "It's really fantastic to be here with you lot,' I said, "and I don't ever want anything to change. It's a real pity that they're trying to close the school, and we've got to try to stop them." There were murmurs of agreement all round, even from Dad.

"And there's something else," I continued. "I want to say how fantastic the last year or so has been. I used to make fun of Doug and church and all that. But I changed my mind. And since I became a Christian, even though I've made a bit of a mess of it sometimes, it's really been . . . fantastic." I felt a bit silly — it was the first time I had said anything like that in public — but that was how I felt. Just at that moment I really felt great!

We finished off the party with some games.

We played musical knees, which was hysterical. Half those playing go one way round to find a chair when the music stops, the others go the other way and sit on the knees of those on the chairs. I was doing great, except for the fact that Sam somehow kept finishing up on my knees, which made everybody laugh except Sam and me. I kept thinking how I could get my own back on

Doug, who was working the music and choosing when to stop it!

However, eventually it got down to one chair, with Raj and me going one way, and Lump and Whizzer going the other. We paced round two other chairs spread out to make it more difficult.

The music stopped.

I hurtled round and made it to the chair before Raj.

The prize was a big bar of chocolate, enough to make Lump careless and keen to win! He made a dash for my knees, trying to get there before Whizzer, who was pretty fast. This was going to be painful!

Lump was in the lead, closely followed by Whizzer.

You may remember the jelly Lump dropped. This was when he found it again. Just before he reached me, taking a wider path because of his speed, his front foot hit the jelly. Instead of landing in a bone-crunching way on his knees, he sailed past with a panicky look on his face, straight into what was left of the food table. There was a tremendous "C-RASH".

Food, paper plates and plastic cutlery flew everywhere.

Everything went quiet. Lump groaned.

"I've done it again, haven't I?" he wailed, covered all over with leftovers.

"You sure have," Doug replied, shaking his head.

Then Grandad started to laugh.

"I haven't seen anything as funny as that since Aunty Betty fell off the pier at Blackpool," he said — and everyone fell about in uncontrollable, side-aching laughter!

14

Mo Saves the Day

I couldn't get over my birthday. It was the best ever. Even Ram wished me a happy birthday!

I rode my bike around, showing it off to anybody who wanted to know, and a good few who didn't. There was plenty of practice to be done as well before the cycle race the following Saturday.

Ram was having a bad week. His team was disqualified by Mr Bolton from the cycle race because Bolthead reckoned their bikes weren't fit. They *were* a bit ropey, but not that bad. I think the fact that the windows of Mr Bolton's shop were daubed with white paint, saying SAVE OUR SCHOOL and DOWN WITH BOLTON, may have had something to do with it. Ram and his mates had been caught "white handed". He got into awful trouble. The police were called and the gang got a ticking-off at the police station. And they were suspended from school for a week. I felt really sorry for them, even though it was Ram. I knew what they were going through, I had been there myself!

I could have told him that wasn't the best way of doing things, but I knew he wouldn't have listened. I hadn't either.

We had a new lad in class — "Scuffer", from Liverpool. And before Ram knew it, all his mates had joined up with Scuffer. Some pals they were! Scuffer looked a real nutcase, ready to cause bother with anybody who argued with him. I could see trouble ahead!

The Saturday of the cycle race came, and we all gathered at the park — the scene of many triumphs and disasters over the years.

Lots of the kids in the race had SOS on their shirts. It really got Mr Bolton wound up, I could see, but there was nothing he could do about it. We'd painted it in red on old white T-shirts. My mum had helped to do it and it really stood out.

We also called ourselves the SOS team.

The race was a sort of relay. Two cyclists from each team began, and the fastest one set off the next two in the team, and so on. The team's time was taken from its first member past the winning post. Very complicated, but that's the way grown-ups like it!

After a lot of fussing about by Mr Bolton, everything was just about ready to start. He spent ages trying to get the right photo for the press (with as little of the SOS stuff showing as possible) but eventually gave up and made the best of it.

He made sure his own ugly mug would be plastered all over the local press, giving himself plenty of free publicity. He wasn't running this race for our sake. He also made sure that his own sponsored team got their picture taken, all equipment courtesy of "Bolton's Cycles". But I didn't care, I was on my new bike in my new gear, courtesy of my family and friends, and that was much better.

Sparky and Whizzer were starting for our team, with each lap of the relay taking one circuit of the park — a shorter one than the kart race, thank goodness. The route was round the lake, through the wood, and across the football pitches.

With a great flourish, Bolton waved a big Union Jack and the race was on. Sparky and Whizzer set off among the pack, heading for the lake. For once we had persuaded Whizzer to leave his headphones behind, so he could concentrate. "No problem, man," was his response to my encouragement before the start. I hoped he was right!

I could see across the lake that Sparky was up near the front, with Whizzer somewhere in the middle. Then they disappeared into the trees.

Looking round I could see Ram leaning on his bike at the side watching. He gave me a thumbs-up sign. Boy, was that guy changing! Then I noticed a huge black eye. He looked very lonely without his gang around him.

Then it was back to the race, and no Sparky. He'd had a puncture in the woods, so it was up to Whizzer.

Seeing what had happened, Whizzer was really turning it on. His feet were whizzing round so fast they were a blur. He came hurtling across the field in third place. He was trying so hard that, as usual, he didn't think about stopping. He crossed the line and Chip and Raj set off after the leader, who was from Bolton's team of course.

Whizzer meanwhile was forced to a halt by the bush he collided with! It took him ten minutes to get both himself and his bike out, and he also got a mouthful from a very unhappy park-keeper!

Bolton was giving a running commentary to a bored-looking local news reporter about how he wanted to help local kids so much, and explaining that he had bought all the kit for his team and got Mr Pick to coach them "to set an example and a standard to the others".

Rhubarb!

Mr Pick was there with his clipboard and stop-watch, yelling orders to his team, who looked frightened to death of losing.

Raj was strong and fast, and good at every-thing. I was really impressed with Raj. People teased him about his colour — and he answered the best way he could. He never said much, but beat them at everything!

But Chip was slower. He was brilliant at maths, but not always that good at practical things. He made them too complicated. His bike had so many gadgets, he had no chance of going fast. He had everything from wing mirrors to a special speedometer and stop-watch. The trouble was, he spent so much time checking his gadgets that he was prone to accidents!

As Raj gradually caught up with the leader, round the back of the lake — with us cheering and shouting like lunatics — Chip fell back to nearly last. Into the woods they shot, and we all waited with bated breath.

Out from the woods hurtled the leader. It was Raj!

I looked across at Bolton and Pick. They weren't pleased. Their guy was following in second place.

I made sure that Lump and Sam were ready to go. There was no sign of Chip.

It was time for dirty tricks! As Raj had taken the lead, there was some jostling for position at the take-over point and, just as Sam was about to set off, one of Bolton's team crossed in front of her.

"Hey," I yelled. "Get out of the way."

But it all happened too quickly. Instead of Sam setting off first, Lump and the other member of Bolton's team did.

Lump wasn't in this race because he wanted to be. Everyone had to take part because we needed eight riders. Even Mo was pressed into service to make up the numbers. She was racing with me on the last circuit.

As it was, Lump was soon passed and Sam tucked into third place behind the two from Bolton's team. The other teams were bunching up behind. As they rounded the lake, Sam was beginning to overtake the others. She was very fast over short distances, and looked after her bike, so she was really zooming. Somehow, as she passed the lad who had blocked her at the start, he sort of swerved, missed his pedal, and cartwheeled beautifully into the lake. Never tangle with Sam. It's not a good idea!

Bolton and Pick weren't amused, but the rest of us thought it was hilarious!

Lump was trailing along behind, trying to open a chocolate bar to keep him going, and didn't notice the bend at the same spot. With great precision he drove straight on and into the lake, just as the lad was getting out. Lump's bike stopped at the mud, and he flew straight on into the arms of the emerging cyclist. They both returned to the water, held in each other's arms, with Lump on top. Lump and water attracted each other like magnets. He knew more ways to fall into it than Wally knew to beg for biscuits. It was incredible!

They dragged themselves out, covered in mud and water, crossed the path and sat down. Meanwhile Sam was crossing the field in the lead. What a fantastic effort.

I was getting ready for the start, with Mo at my side. I smiled down at her, and she smiled nervously back. It was the first time she had joined us in one of our competitions and she didn't want to get it wrong. We were off. Racing against us from Bolton's team were two of the best athletes from school. I would have to do really well to beat them.

Mo fell behind as we approached the lake, and my two competitors were up alongside me.

I remembered from the kart race that the path was quite narrow as it went round the back of the lake. Just at this point these two big lads leaned their bikes across to fill the path. There was nothing I could do. I had to brake and let them in.

Now I was tucked in behind them, and the second one slowed down to block me and let the leader get away. Talk about dirty tricks. That Pick had taught them well! There was nothing I could do, but up ahead things were happening.

Ram had made his way round to where Lump was sitting. The track just there was now covered in mud and water, making it very slippy. When the guy in the lead reached that point his wheels slipped from under him, and he fell right across the path. His team-mate couldn't stop and ran straight into him. I skidded to the side, on to the grass and fell off. Then the rest of the cyclists slid gently into the growing heap.

Ram was helping sort out the tangle, but it looked to me as if he was making it worse, and he had a wicked grin on his face as he kept saying "sorry" and "please let me help"!

The only one not to fall was — Mo! She cycled up to the writhing heap, wheeled her bike round, and cycled on.

"Go, Mo, go!" I yelled.

She just put her head down and set off on her

little bike. She disappeared into the woods before we had sorted ourselves out, with Ram's help. He gave me a big wink from his blackened eye. I tried to get my bike going, but the chain had jammed and I could only wheel it back towards the start and hope.

Mo shot out of the woods in the lead and was half way back across the field before anybody appeared.

The two guys from Bolton's team shot out in pursuit, and were making ground all the time.

Everybody except Bolton's team was shouting for Mo. She had her head down and was cycling as hard as ever she could, her little legs whirling round like mad. My mum and dad had arrived and they were shouting and screaming for her.

As the finishing line drew nearer, so did the other cyclists, but Mo hurtled to the line and just made it, by half a wheel. Brilliant! Cool! Wicked!

Dad carried her round on his shoulders, he was so proud.

Bolton and Pick looked as if someone was standing on their toes.

I made Mo collect the trophy. She was so delighted. Mr Bolton wasn't. He had to hand over the trophy to Mo, who had a big red SOS on her T-shirt, and have his photograph taken giving her some vouchers to spend in his shop. What a humiliation!

What a triumph!

Dad carried Mo all the way home!

15

Nick & Co. Close In

On Monday at school the new kid, Scuffer, was throwing his weight about, but I wasn't interested. That sort of thing didn't really bother me any more. I was sick of fighting and arguing!

Poor Ram was looking awful. His old pals were just smirking at him and making comments. How are the mighty fallen!

We found out that Ram had got his black eye in a scrap with Scuffer. I wondered how long Scuffer would last before he got in real bother. He didn't seem particularly interested in getting at me maybe because I didn't rise when he tried to wind me up. This was the new Nick!

Ram spent most of the lunch-time sitting on the school wall, looking lonely and sad. Sparky went across for a chat, then came over to me.

"I . . . er . . . asked him if he'd liked to join our club," he said nervously.

I was just about to say something really nasty, when I stopped myself. Ram had helped in the cycle race, and he did seem to be trying. Just as long as he didn't try to take over.

"OK, we'll give him a try," I responded.

"Great," Sparky said, with a certain amount of relief and amazement in his voice.

That night after school we were going to Bolton's cycle shop to spend the vouchers we had won. Sam, Sparky, Whizzer, Raj and I had been elected to choose.

When we arrived, Bolton was in a really funny mood. He had been talking to some people in the shop, but immediately shut up when we walked in.

"Oh, not you lot," was Bolton's response to us. "Can't you come another time?"

We didn't move.

"Well," he went on. "I suppose it's best to get it over with. Do you know what you want?"

We didn't really know what to get with the fifty pounds' worth of vouchers, so we asked if we could look round.

"Oh, all right," was Bolton's reluctant response. "But don't be long about it." He ushered the other people into the office at the back of the shop and left us to it.

We all split up to see what Bolton had to offer. I was looking around near the counter when I noticed some papers. Being a nosey sort of a person I couldn't resist looking to see what they were. They were copies of some sort of plans. Then the penny dropped. They were plans for the site of our school. I was just about to have

114

a closer look when I heard Bolton coming back. Making an instant decision, I grabbed one of the plans, pushed it under my shirt and quickly moved away, pretending to look at some caps. Bolton went straight to the plans, grabbed them and, with a guilty look on his face, took them to his office.

"What shall we get?" Sam asked. "I've seen loads of stuff which we could use on our bikes."

"Yes," Whizzer added. "And there are some great caps and gloves and that sort of thing."

"Fine," I responded. "You choose, I . . . er . . . I've got to go somewhere. I'll see you at the hut.'

They all stood there with their mouths open as I walked out. I left the shop at a gentle stroll, trying to look as though I was in no sort of a hurry. As soon as I was round the corner I ran as fast as I could towards home.

When I got to my room I retrieved the plan from under my shirt and straightened it out. It showed the area of the school and Bolton's shop, with drawings for some shops and a big sports club. So that was what Bolton was up to. I knew he was a crook! What was I going to do now? How should I deal with this information? How long before Bolton discovered it was missing and did something? I decided to go to the club hut to tell the others.

Ram was already waiting outside the hut when I got there. Doug wasn't coming and I had the key. I let us both in and almost straight away the others arrived, then Lump and Chip, and Mo, who had followed me from home with Wally. While everyone looked at the prizes from Bolton's shop — caps and things to stick on our bikes — Sparky pulled me to one side.

"Why did you cut off so mysteriously?" he asked.

I told him about the plans and he looked shocked.

"You shouldn't have stolen them," he said.

"I had to do something," I grunted back.

"Yes, but stealing?" he went on.

I agreed to show Doug and ask his advice, but then we were interrupted by Ram. What he told us immediately set us on another track.

"You know I saw you chasing a bloke with your dog the other day," he began.

"Yes," I replied, grateful for the change of subject.

"Well," he went on. "When I was watching the cycle race I saw the same bloke going into a house at the back of the park by the lake."

Ram was obviously trying to get well in with us, and I was a bit suspicious about what he said, but there was no reason why we shouldn't check it out. I told the rest of the gang and we set off to the park.

On the way I talked to Ram. "I don't want you to get the wrong idea, Ram," I said sternly. "After all that's happened between us, I need some real proof before I can trust you as a proper member of our club." He couldn't argue with that; after all, he had nobody else now.

We reached the park, and I told everybody to wait there under Sparky's orders until I called them.

Ram, Sam, Raj and I went on to the house Ram pointed out to us. Super sleuth, ace detective, Nick Baker goes into action yet again for the cause of good, defeating evil. If there had been a spare telephone box I could have donned my Superman outfit, but plain old jeans and T-shirt would have to do! We crept up to the house, which faced the park.

"How do we know he lives here?" Raj whispered. "He could have been just visiting."

I gave him a shut up look, I didn't want questions like that now.

We waited for ages, and I was just about to give up on Ram, when Sam grabbed my arm. She pointed to the house. Someone was coming out.

It was the man! He was wearing that same, grotty old coat. He turned up the street.

I turned to Raj. "Tell the others to meet us at the corner of Seddon Street, and to keep hidden," I ordered.

He crept off. I knew that the man would have to go past that corner. We would follow him. I didn't know why — it was the only thing I could think of to do. Sam, Ram and I followed the bloke, keeping a safe distance. Sure enough, he went in the direction I had thought.

At the corner of Seddon Street, Sparky and Whizzer were innocently playing with a ball. The man walked past them without a glance.

Suddenly we were grabbed into an alleyway. The rest of the gang were there. Sparky and Whizzer joined us.

"What now?" Sparky asked.

"We follow him some more," I replied. "But well spread out."

I set off and the others followed at safe distances, with Mo and Wally at the rear. We had gone up and down several streets without any sort of purpose when suddenly the man stopped, looked at a piece of paper, and turned up a path to a house. It was old Mrs Brogan's from church.

I had to do something quickly. By the time we reached the house he had talked his way in. I gathered everybody round.

"Whizzer, Lump, and Chip. Round the back to see if he tries to get out that way," I ordered. "Sparky, go and ring my dad at the police station. He'll believe you! Mo, you'd better go round the back, out of the way, with Wally, too. The rest of us will wait at the front. Spread yourselves out!"

They all went to their places. Sparky hurtled off. I hoped he wouldn't be long. Then things went wrong!

We must have disturbed him. He had grabbed the old lady's handbag and pushed her down, making her cry out. I didn't want Mrs Brogan getting hurt — apart from anything else, she made the best cakes in church!

The man poked his head round the front door and saw the three of us. He decided to escape at the back, rather than have another chase.

We hurtled round to the back.

"Where is he?" I demanded of those waiting there.

"Where's who?" was Lump's reply. "No one's come out here."

"You've not missed him, you plonkers?" I moaned.

"No, we haven't," Chip replied. "We were watching carefully."

"I've seen that before," I responded.

Then Wally took over. He slipped his lead and headed for Mrs Brogan's back yard. We chased after him. He went straight for Mrs Brogan's outside toilet and stopped, barking furiously. Sam twigged straight away, and grabbed a dustbin, shoving it against the toilet door.

"What are you doing?" I demanded.

Sam pointed to the door. I looked at her, thinking she had flipped.

Suddenly there was a terrific banging and the door started to move. The man was in there! I grabbed Lump and shoved him against the door. Then we all piled up round him.

"Gerroff, gerroff, you're hurting," Lump wailed.

"I'll get you lot," screamed the man from inside the toilet.

"Mo, go and see if Mrs Brogan is all right," I yelled, and she dashed into the house.

Would we hold out till Dad came?

16

Mission Complete

"Open this door," the man demanded, shouting and screaming from inside the toilet.

"Do something," Lump wailed. He was pressed against the door by the rest of us and every time the door was thumped from the inside, he got the full force of it.

"Oh, Mum," he wailed after a particularly hard bang. The door was beginning to break up!

"Hold on," I yelled. "Somebody will soon be here."

It was time for another of those silent prayers for help.

The man had punched a hole at the top of the door and his hand was reaching through. Lump was ducking and weaving his head to avoid the man grabbing it. He couldn't move anything else; we were pushing against him. To add to the mayhem, Wally was barking for all he was worth. "Help! help!" Lump yelled, as the man nearly grabbed him.

Just as the bloke's hand was coming round for

120

another go, Sam made her mark. She reached up, grabbed his arm, and bit! Boy, did he yell!

After that he went back to throwing himself at the door. Just when we thought we'd had it, there was the sound of a police siren.

"About time," I shouted. "Hang on folks, not much longer."

Things happened fast. Dad and several of his mates piled out of a van, ran round to us, and waited while we moved out of the way.

Suddenly it all went quiet.

The man thumped the door and it flew open. His anger turned to a look of shocked surprise when he saw six huge policemen standing shoulder to shoulder. He didn't argue! He was bundled into the van and driven away.

Mrs Brogan was OK; Mo had made her a cup of tea.

We had to make statements, but we were getting used to this!

At tea that night Mum asked us all about it and we told her.

"You did very well," Dad said. "But I do sometimes wish I had an ordinary son who did normal things like playing in the park, and left crime-fighting to the experts."

"Look, Dad," I replied. "I don't go out searching for these things. They sort of find me."

He had a disbelieving look on his face.

"Just make sure you stay the right side of the law,' he warned. "I don't want you getting involved with breaking into premises or taking things that don't belong to you."

I nearly choked on my chips. With great difficulty I changed the subject. I was very glad when the meal was over and I could escape to my room. I'd begun to realize the spot I had got myself into. I needed to talk to Doug!

Fortunately I had no homework, so I was able to go round that evening. I tried his home, but he wasn't there. Then I tried the church. It was a bit creepy going in when it was empty. Usually when I was there it was full of people.

Doug was doing some work, and I made him jump when I popped my head round the door to the vestry room at the back. "Hello Nick," he said. "What are you doing here?"

"Er, can we talk?" I mumbled.

He put down what he was doing.

"Come on in and pull up a chair," he responded. What a guy! I don't think he'd ever turn anyone away.

It all went quiet.

He waited.

So I told him all about catching the man.

He listened.

"That's great," he said. "But that's not what you want to talk about, is it?"

How did he know?

I pulled the plan out from under my shirt and put it on the desk. He looked at it.

"Where did you get this?" he asked.

I told him.

"Hmm," he mumbled.

"Before you say anything," I went on. "I realize it was wrong to take it. I just acted on an impulse and, after all, Bolton's doing something really wicked."

"Hmm," he mumbled again.

"I know, I know," I continued. "Two wrongs don't make a right."

He raised his eyebrows.

"I could always sneak it back on to his counter," I added.

He looked at me.

I looked back at him.

"So what do I do?" I finally said. "My dad'll kill me when he finds out!"

Doug is amazing. He knew just what to do. After a pause to think he replied. "*You* don't take it back, *we* do," he responded. "And, depending on what happens, I'll see your dad and anyone else who needs to know."

Before I left, we prayed together about what we were going to do and I felt much better.

The next day, after school, Doug met me with the plans and we went to Bolton's shop.

"Well, what do you want?" Bolton demanded.

As Doug told him what I had done and handed over the plans, I saw Mr Bolton's expression change from embarrassment to anger to worry.

I could feel the blood draining from my legs. I wanted to be somewhere, anywhere else!

"I shouldn't have taken them and I'm sorry," I stammered out. I really meant it!

"You young hooligan," Bolton steamed at me. "How dare you do such a thing? You should be ashamed of yourself."

"We all do things we should be ashamed of sometimes!" Doug cut in. That was clever. I wished I could have thought of that. It really shut Bolton up.

Then they made me wait outside. Looking through the window, I could see Bolton going on at a very calm Doug. I think Bolton was trying to persuade him to hush things up. Then Bolton stormed off to the back of his shop and Doug came out.

"Phew!" was the only comment Doug would make. What a bloke!

Doug came home with me and we explained things again to Dad. He wasn't too pleased with me for taking the plan, especially after his little lecture at the tea-table the other evening. But he was very interested in all the details of the plan which Doug told him about.

When Doug had gone I got another of those lectures. I did my bit and was ever so sorry and all that sort of stuff. It's one of those sort of rituals in life that have to happen, I guess. It would be nice if it happened the other way round a few times. Why don't dads ever do anything wrong? They only have what they call "slight miscalculations"! Either that, or it was somebody else's fault in the first place.

The next day at school, word was getting

round. Kids kept asking me what it was all about.

Even Scuffer stopped thumping people briefly to find out what was going on before going back to making Ram's life, in particular, a misery. More and more, Ram was taking protection in our gang. I think he actually enjoyed it. He even started smartening himself up a bit. The only thing I didn't like was the fuss he was making of Sam!

I was called to the Head's office again. I guessed it was for another ticking off. Bolton would probably have fed him his version, and I would get expelled or something.

I knocked on the door and waited for the dreaded call.

The door opened.

"Come in, come in young man," Potty said, as if I was royalty. Gordon Bennett, I didn't expect that! "Well now, young man," Potty went on. "You've been up to things again, haven't you?"

I nodded, confused by his attitude.

"You shouldn't have done that really, should you?" he continued.

"Er . . . no," I replied.

"Off you go then," he concluded.

My mouth dropped open. He must have flipped. I headed for the door.

"Oh, by the way," he added as I reached the door. "I was on the phone to the local council this morning. For some reason the school is going to stay open after all. Good news isn't it?" There was a distinct twinkle in his eye.

I beamed!

As I wandered back to class I looked out of the window and saw Doug getting back into his battered old van. So that's what had happened. Good old Doug had sorted things out in his no fuss, no problem way. What a guy!

Mr Bolton, of course, resigned as chairperson of the school governors, and we never saw him again in school. His shop was also closed — until someone else took it over. My dad said that the Fraud Squad were looking into some of Bolton's activities. It was a real scandal! I was just glad that he was out of our hair.

It was another case of Nick Baker crime-fighter, solver of mysteries and general genius!

I was also amazed that Ram continued to join in. He had even started going to church. At school he didn't say much, but kept very close to the rest of us. Every time he was on his own, Scuffer and Ram's old gang had a go at him.

Scuffer couldn't make *me* out! I wouldn't get into a fight with him. That's not the new Nick's style. And, anyway, he was such a great big bloke, I wouldn't have won. I'd have to find another way to put him in his place.

After school I was making my way home, telling the gang all about my do with Potty, when Ram came hurtling round the corner. "They're after me," he gasped, looking helpless.

I groaned inside. Just at that moment I didn't want to get involved in Ram's problems. Why should I help, after all he'd done to me? I didn't need Doug to tell me that as a Christian I couldn't turn away and ignore him. But I also knew that if we got involved, we would all get thumped. Scuffer was too big and too tough.

At that moment the big, ugly, vicious Scuffer came round the corner, followed by his new gang. He looked mean and nasty.

I looked round at my pals, who looked as nervous as I felt. Now what?

17

Another New Member

"Where is he?" Scuffer demanded.

We stood in a bunch by a low wall. Ram lay flat behind the wall.

Should I lie? Should I tell the truth? It was another time for a swift prayer for help. Don't get me wrong, I don't just pray when I'm desperate, but it's certainly useful in situations like this!

Inspiration struck. "Ah Scuffer," I began, changing the subject. "I was meaning to have a chat with you."

"Uh?" he grunted, confused.

"I wanted officially to welcome you to our school and to offer my assistance should you require it in order to find out where all the necessary things are."

He stood with his mouth slightly open.

"You may not know this, but in the past I have been the top man around here," I continued. "However, as you are obviously so superior in all sorts of ways, both mentally and physically, it is obvious that you should take over."

He nearly smiled. His chest puffed out. He turned to his pals, nodded, and strutted off down the road.

We waited for him to turn the corner.

"What a Wally," I said to no one in particular.

We all fell about laughing, and Ram clambered out from his hiding-place. It had taken me a long time to find it out, but there really are much better ways of sorting things out than getting angry.

The next day at school was really embarrassing. During assembly the gang was called up on to the stage while Mr Potter told the school about how we had captured the man who had been robbing the old folks. We all stood there shuffling while he told the tale.

Looking across at the staff, I was disappointed not to see Pick there. In fact, when I thought about it, he hadn't been around for a few days. He was a bit nasty, but surely he wasn't involved in Bolton's set up? We soon got the answer. At the end of assembly, Mr Potter announced that Mr Pick would be absent for the next week or so. He had injured his foot falling off his bicycle. I know we shouldn't have laughed, but the whole school fell about. Even the staff joined in.

Back in the classroom, Scuffer was not looking pleased. However hard he pushed his weight about, I still seemed to win out. I just can't see why people think violence and making the loudest noise could ever win in the end!

Miss Nolan came in and settled us down eventually. "If this goes on much longer we'll have to widen the doors," she commented.

I looked puzzled.

"You'll never get your head through them as they are!" she added sarcastically.

What a put down, and after all I'd done to save the school.

Charming!

Doug had more good news for us that evening at the club. Not only was the school staying open, there was also a strong possibility that a new sports centre would be built on the site, to make it into a sort of "Community School".

That sounded great!

We settled down to our club evening, playing loads of games. I had just started a game of darts with Raj when the door opened and in came Bert.

"Hello," Sam greeted him. "What are you doing here?"

"I invited him," Doug responded.

Bert looked around, then made for a comfy chair.

"It's a bit noisy," he complained. That's my Bert! However, he soon settled down to a game of dominoes with Lump and Chip.

I wandered over after slamming Raj at darts.

Bert looked at me. "When I first met you," he said, "I thought you were a real bad lot."

I looked at him.

"But I was wrong," he added. "Not only did

you catch that devil that was hurting us old folk. You and Ram also helped me to see what a sour old man I had become. When I was younger I used to go to church and all that, but decided it wasn't for me. I think I'll give it another try."

What could I say? I smiled and went over to Doug. When I told him what Bert had said he laughed.

"Good news, eh, Nick," he said. "But don't worry, he's not joining the youth club. I'll take him to the one we run for Senior Citizens."

Before I could say anything else, Ram walked in with Sparky. I still couldn't get used to the new Ram, he'd changed so much.

I played him at pool and we were both trying so hard to "play fair" the whole thing became ridiculous. Then we both got frustrated with this and started playing hard. Soon everybody was watching. I had to win!

Ram was just as bad, it really got nasty.

I looked him in the eye. We tried to outstare each other. But then we totally cracked up. It was so silly! We fell over the table laughing our heads off. All the others thought we had gone totally mad!

At the end of the evening Doug gave us one of his talks. It was about a man in the Bible called Daniel. Foreign soldiers took him from his home when he was just a teenager and he was made to work in another country. They offered him all sorts of goodies if he would forget about God and do what the king said. But Daniel and his pals refused. It was dead hard for him. One time he got thrown into a pit of lions, another time his friends got chucked in a furnace. But in the end, instead of losing out, he became the king's most trusted adviser — a real top dog in the land.

Wow! And all because he wouldn't just do the easy thing, only the *right* thing, in God's way!

"When you do things the way God wants, it's sometimes hard at the time. And you may never be rich or famous, but you still can't lose in the end," Doug concluded. He was right!

We were just about to go when Doug called us back. "Oh, I nearly forgot," he said. "Somebody has given you some money for catching that crook. It's not a fortune. But enough to give us a night out at the ice-skating rink, with refreshments provided."

We were all delighted. Doug wouldn't let on who had given the money, but Bert looked very pleased that we were so happy!

We set a date for Saturday night.

On the Saturday we all turned up at five o'clock to wait for Doug. I was dreading being squashed up in Doug's old van. It would be even more difficult now Ram had joined us. Then came the first surprise. Doug had hired a mini-bus. We travelled in luxury!

The only irritating thing was the fact that Ram sat on the back seat, with Sam between us. What was he up to?

Of course, on the way we had to stop for

Lump to get something to eat. His first bag of chips stank the bus out for the rest of the journey to the rink.

I had never been ice-skating before, but I was sure I could manage it, no problem. I had some old roller skates and could manage to get around on them!

At the stadium we piled out into the car park and made our way inside.

First we had to hire some boots. It took Whizzer three goes before he sorted a pair out. He couldn't remember what size shoes he wore, and he had one foot a size bigger than the other. The boots felt really strange when I eventually stood up. I was beginning to have my doubts about all this.

Sam took my hand — to help me get my balance, you understand! She'd been skating before, so had Sparky.

We wobbled through to the rink.

Loads of people were already there, circling round.

"I don't think I'm going to like this," Chip wailed.

"Nonsense," Doug replied. "Once you get going you'll be all right."

I wasn't so sure.

To begin with I made a fuss of retying my laces, so that I could watch the others having a go. Lump flatly refused to move. Sam and Sparky set off at speed. Whizzer and Raj had a go and wobbled off, quickly getting the hang of it. Next came Chip, who stuck a nervous leg out and was whisked away by Sam and Sparky as they looped round.

"Come on, Nick," they yelled.

Lump still refused to move.

Ram came past me and launched himself out on to the ice. He was good, he'd done it before. The creep hadn't let on, either.

I reached out with one foot, placed it gingerly on the ice then, hanging on to the side, brought the other foot out to join it. It didn't feel good!

People were whizzing past!

I pulled myself along a bit, feeling very weird, with my ankles wobbling from side to side.

Ram whooshed past!

I'd have to do something. I pushed off. It felt great for all of two seconds before my feet decided to go in different directions at a different speed to the rest of my body.

SPLAT!!

18

Pile Up!

Not only is ice hard and cold, it is also wet. It is also very difficult to get up when you fall over. Every time I managed to get half way up, one of my feet would take independent action and shoot off, landing me back on my bottom. It was very frustrating.

Sam and Sparky came along to help, together with Ram. How embarrassing.

I was too proud to accept help. "It's all right. It's all right," I insisted. "I think there must be something wrong with these boots." I crawled to the side and off the ice, my bottom feeling very damp.

Ram, Sparky and Sam skated off, holding hands, with Sam in the middle. Ram looked pleased.

I felt cross. If that Ram was trying to muscle in, something would have to be done. Even if he had "changed". I pretended to retie the laces of my skates!

Doug skated up. He was good too!

"What's up, Nick?" he asked.

"Not a lot," I replied.

"Do you want a lesson?" he added.

I looked at him!

"I only asked," he went on. Rather than go away, he came and sat alongside. We watched as Ram and Sam went past, laughing. I was beginning to get a bit huffy inside.

"It's fantastic how Ram's changed, isn't it?" Doug said.

"Ye-es," I replied.

He sensed my doubt. "Now Nick," he went on. "Do I sense a touch of jealousy creeping in here?"

I blushed.

"Do you remember me telling you Paul's story from the Bible?" Doug replied. "He was chasing around trying to get Christians killed. Then he became a Christian, and he changed straight away. The trouble was, the other Christians were so frightened of him, nobody believed him."

Doug skated off, leaving me in peace.

I looked across the ice. Raj and Whizzer were having a good time. Chip was wobbling about, clutching at the side, and Lump had not moved more than a couple of metres from where he had got on to the ice. He was leaning heavily on the side, looking most unhappy.

Sam and Ram came over. "Come on, Nick," Sam yelled.

"In a minute, in a minute," I grumped.

She muttered something to Ram, who skated off, then she joined me. Sam sat down. "Why don't you just admit you can't skate?" she demanded.

I blushed! How did she know?

She grabbed me by the hand and yanked me to my feet. I hobbled to the edge, and Sam helped me get going. I discovered it was a real advantage being a beginner. You really have to hold on tight to the person helping you! I was beginning to enjoy myself.

Then there was commotion.

Raj and Whizzer had decided to give the unwilling Lump a hand. One on either side, they had started to guide him round. They were both pretty strong lads but when it came to the corner, after gaining a little speed, they couldn't manage to turn him.

Lump went straight on! They lost their grip and all three tumbled to the ice. Then it became like a skittle alley. They mowed down at least ten others, and the whole lot slid in a great seething pile, right into the side.

The hooter went and we all stopped and got off the ice while they sorted things out. It was like untangling string. Lump was last up, wet through and miserable, and complaining bitterly. His sweets were scattered over the ice and were being swept up by the attendants. He grovelled around trying to rescue them.

While everybody got back on the ice, I took Sam for a drink and ice cream. We were just chatting when Sam caught my arm and pointed. Walking into the rink were Scuffer and his pals!

Oh no!

"What are we going to do?" Sam asked.

"What do you mean?" I replied. "Just keep out of his way and there's no problem."

"What about Ram?" she asked.

"That's Ram's problem," I replied. "Or are you more worried about Ram than me?"

I wished I hadn't said that. Sam took her ice cream cornet and pressed it firmly on my nose before walking off! Now I had a cold, wet nose as well as a cold, wet behind. The waitress in the cafe collapsed behind the counter laughing. Glancing in the mirror I looked just like Pinocchio. OK, I was wrong. I just couldn't help myself.

I cleaned myself up and hobbled back to the ice. Lump was standing by the ice and I went alongside. Chip pulled himself round and we all watched as Scuffer passed. He was fantastic, very fast, but a real show-off, doing twists and turns as he skated in between everybody.

He soon saw Ram! He quickly had a word with his pals before setting off after Ram. Every time the attendants at the rink were looking the other way, Scuffer screamed past Ram and gave him a thump. What's more, Ram couldn't get off the ice, because the others in Scuffer's gang were hanging round the exits, pushing him back. It was looking very nasty.

Doug saw what was going on and tried to talk

to Scuffer, but he just got pushed away, banging into the side.

Oh well, I guessed it was up to me to think of something. I watched Scuffer looping round, cutting across Ram, and catching him with his elbows or hands. Sam and Sparky were trying to protect him and getting hurt themselves.

It was time for the secret weapon. I edged up behind Lump. If I had told him what I was going to do, he would never have let me. As Scuffer was coming past I gave Lump a shove. He shot out on to the ice towards Scuffer, arms and legs waving in all directions. The crash was inevitable.

Right at the last moment, as Lump had now fallen and was sliding along on his back, Scuffer made an incredible leap and went right over him. The trouble was, in shoving Lump I had pushed myself out as well, clutching at Chip for help. As we were both hopeless at skating, that wasn't much use.

Scuffer cleared Lump all right, but straight after landing collided with Chip and me. The lights went out in my head.

I came round in the first-aid room, in the arms of Sam. Was I in heaven?

Everyone was really making a fuss of me. Scuffer had been thrown out after Doug explained to the attendants what had been happening.

I had to go to hospital for a check-up, but I was all right.

"A head like concrete," Doug said to the doctor.

Thanks a bunch, I thought.

Mum and Dad came to the hospital to pick me up. They knew the way — I had been there many times before. There wasn't a lot Dad could say. I think he had given up trying!

Mo and Wally were in the car and my sore head got a real licking from my daft pet.

The next day, Ram's parents came round with some chocolates. That was kind, and it didn't take long for me to polish them off. It was a Sunday, and Ram was taking his parents to church. He really had changed!

On Monday at school, Ram never left my side, it was embarrassing. Then I realized why. Scuffer was waiting for me.

The whole gang rallied round, so Scuffer couldn't get to me. He got so frustrated that he eventually confronted me in class. To the astonishment of Miss Nolan, he got up, walked over to my desk, grabbed me by the jacket and snarled into my face, "I'll get you for Saturday. You'll regret what you did. More than you can imagine."

He totally ignored Miss Nolan, but fortunately Mr Pick was hobbling past. He hopped into the room and dragged Scuffer out in the direction of the Head's office. He wasn't such a bad guy after all!

I knew that Scuffer would be back. No sooner was one problem sorted than another one began. Why does it always happen to me?

At break I gathered the gang round. "OK, folks," I said. "This Scuffer problem. I think I have a plan."

Lump groaned!

NICK & CO. IN A FIX

Bob Croson

Trouble never seems to be far away when the irrepressible Nick Baker is around. No matter how good his intentions, Nick's brainwaves always seem to backfire, with unexpected and often hilarious results.

When Nick and Co. hear that a local business-man is threatening to close down their youth club, they decide to take action. But Nick's Master Plan doesn't turn out quite as they had expected...

ISBN 0 85648 953 0

NICK & CO. ON HOLIDAY

Bob Croson

When Nick & Co. go camping it's a riot from start to finish. The gang's arrival certainly livens up the sleepy little country village of Tidesbourne. And before long Nick & Co. find themselves in the middle of an adventure.

What is Old Tom's secret?

And who are the mysterious sheep-stealers?

Nick & Co. are on the trail again.

ISBN 0 7459 1346 6

More stories from LION PUBLISHING for you to enjoy:

Adventures

NICK AND CO. ON HOLIDAY Bob Croson	£2.99☐
NICK AND CO. TO THE RESCUE Bob Croson	£2.99☐
KATE AND THE MYSTERY PONIES	
Sally Fielding	£2.75☐
KATE AND THE HORRIBLE HORSE	
Sally Fielding	£2.50☐
SWEET 'N' SOUR SUMMER Janice Brown	£2.50☐
MYSTERY AT HAWKTOWERS Chris Spencer	£2.25☐

Science Fiction

OPERATION TITAN Dilwyn Horvat	£2.50☐
ASSAULT ON OMEGA FOUR Dilwyn Horvat	£2.50☐
STARFORCE RED ALERT Chris Spencer	£2.50☐

All Lion paperbacks are available from your local bookshop or news-agent, or can be ordered direct from the address below. Just tick the titles you want and fill in the form.

Name (Block letters)_____

Address_____

_____

Write to Lion Publishing, Cash Sales Department, PO Box 11, Falmouth, Cornwall TR10 9EN, England.

Please enclose a cheque or postal order to the value of the cover price plus:

UK INCLUDING BFPO: £1.00 for the first book, 50p for the second book and 30p for each additional book ordered to a maximum charge of £3.00.

OVERSEAS INCLUDING EIRE: £2.00 for the first book, £1.00 for the second book and 50p for each additional book.

Lion Publishing reserves the right to show on covers and charge new retail prices which may differ from those previously advertised in the text or elsewhere, and to increase postal rates in accordance with the Post Office.